LUCY DANIELS

Animal Ark Pets™

Chick Challenge
Hamster Hotel
Mouse Magic

*Hodder
Children's
Books*

A division of Hachette Children's Books

Animal Ark Pets™

Hamster Hotel

Special thanks to Sue Welford
Thanks to C. J, Hall, B.Vet.Med., M.R.C.V.S., for reviewing
the veterinary material contained in this book.

This edition of Hamster Hotel, Mouse Magic and Chick Challenge
first published in 1998

This edition published in 2008

ISBN-13: 978 0 340 95684 7

Hamster Hotel

Special thanks to Sue Welford

Animal Ark Pets is a registered trademark of Working Partners Ltd.
Text copyright © 1996 Working Partners Ltd.
Created by Working Partners Limited, London W6 0QT
Original series created by Ben M. Baglio
Illustrations copyright © 1996 Paul Howard
Cover illustration by Chris Chapman

The right of Lucy Daniels to be identified as the Author of
the Work has been asserted by her in accordance with the
Copyright, Designs and Patents Act 1988.

For more information about Animal Ark
please contact www.animalark.co.uk

1

A Catalogue record for this book is available from the British Library

Typeset in Bembo by Avon DataSet Ltd, Bidford-on-Avon, Warwickshire

Printed and bound in Great Britain by
Clays Ltd, St Ives plc, Bungay, Suffolk

The paper and board used in this paperback by Hodder Children's
Books are natural recyclable products made from wood grown in
sustainable forests. The manufacturing processes conform to the
environmental regulations of the country of origin.

Hodder Children's Books
a division of Hachette Children's Books
338 Euston Road, London NW1 3BH
An Hachette Livre UK Company

Contents

1

A visitor at Lilac Cottage

"Mandy Hope, did you hear what I said?" Mrs Todd was standing right beside Mandy's school desk.

Mandy looked up at her teacher. She had been miles away. Today was the day that her grandmother's friend Mary was bringing her hamster to stay at Lilac Cottage, the house where Gran lived.

Mandy's grandparents were going to look after the hamster for a week while Mary was away on holiday and Mandy just couldn't wait to meet him.

"Oh, sorry, Mrs Todd," she said. "Er . . . no I didn't."

"What's the heaviest land animal in the world, next to the elephant, Mandy?"

The class were having a quiz and it was Mandy's turn to answer a question.

"Oh," Mandy said. "A rhinoceros."

You could ask Mandy anything about animals and she almost always knew the answer.

Mrs Todd nodded. "Good. Well done, Mandy!"

Mandy glanced up at the clock. Nearly three o'clock. Almost time to go home. Better still, it was half-term. She and her best friend, James Hunter, would have a whole week to spend with the hamster. James was a year younger than Mandy and loved animals almost as much as she did.

James had two pets. A Labrador puppy named Blackie and a cat called Benji.

Mandy would have loved to have a pet too, but her parents were both vets and were too busy looking after other people's animals to have pets of their own.

Mandy wanted to be a vet like her parents one day. She longed to help out with the sick animals at their surgery, Animal Ark, but knew she would have to wait until she was older.

When school had finished, Mandy helped Mrs Todd take Terry and Jerry, the class gerbils, out to her car. Mrs Todd was going to care for them at her house during the holiday.

Mandy said goodbye to Mrs Todd, then ran to meet James who was waiting by the school gate. They always went home together.

"Today's hamster day!" Mandy zipped up her coat against the cold wind.

James pushed his glasses on to the bridge of his nose. "I hadn't forgotten," he said. "When can I come and see him?"

"Mum said I could go straight to Gran's

after school," Mandy said. "You could come with me now if you like."

"Will your gran mind?" James asked.

"Of course she won't," said Mandy.

"Great!" said James, hurrying to keep up. "Let me just tell Mum where I'm going."

He ran on ahead to his house.

"Don't be long," Mandy called. "And better not bring Blackie this time — he might frighten the hamster."

James disappeared into his house.

Mandy waited for him by the front gate. Suddenly a black nose pushed the back door open and Blackie came scampering out. James followed soon after.

"Blackie!" James shouted. "Come back."

Blackie threw himself at Mandy, all big paws and wagging tail. Mandy laughed and gave him a cuddle. Blackie rolled over on his back with his legs in the air so Mandy could tickle his tummy.

James caught up with them and grabbed the puppy's collar. "Blackie, *when* will you learn to do as you're told?" He shook the puppy gently and scolded him. "He's learned to open the door," James explained to Mandy.

"So I see," she chuckled.

Blackie stood up and began licking her face. Mandy gave him another hug. "You're a very clever dog," she said.

"Yes, he is, but when is he going to behave?" said James.

"Never, by the looks of it." Mandy pushed Blackie gently away. "You'll have to take him to proper puppy training classes."

"Dad's already taken him," James told her as he hauled Blackie back into the house. "But he caused a riot."

Mandy chuckled. "A riot?"

"Yes. He ran off with the trainer's whistle, pinched the biscuits they were going to have at break time and got hold of a lady's scarf and tore it to bits. Dad won't take him again."

"I'm not surprised." Mandy burst out laughing. "One of our holiday jobs will have to be some serious training with Blackie," she said.

James looked glum. "We can try," he said.

"But I don't hold out much hope – he hasn't improved much since the last time we tried."

Mandy skipped ahead as they made their way across the village green. It was a damp afternoon, with a hint of drizzle in the wind. "Come on, I can't wait to see the hamster!"

Grandad was busy in the garden of Lilac Cottage, pruning back the shrubs. The sleeves of his old gardening jumper were pushed up to the elbows. There was a wheelbarrow full of twigs and leaves on the path. Mandy pushed past it and ran to give him a hug.

"Come to see Frisky, the hamster?" Grandad asked.

"Yep. I've brought James."

"Jolly good," Grandad said. "Hello, James. How are you?"

"Fine, thank you, Mr Hope," James said.

"That's good. Go on in, Gran's in her study typing some letters."

"Gran, I'm here!" Mandy called as she and James went in through the back door.

The click-clack of Gran's old-fashioned typewriter came from the other room. "James is with me."

Mandy looked round the kitchen. There was no sign of the hamster. They went through into Gran's study.

"Hello, you two," Gran said.

Mandy gave her gran a kiss. "Where is he, Gran?"

Gran turned round in her chair and took off her glasses. "If you mean Frisky, I've put him in the spare room. It's nice and light, and warm by the radiator."

"May we go up and see him, please?"

"Of course you can."

Mandy dumped her bag on the floor and ran up the stairs, James close behind. She pushed open the spare bedroom door. On a little table near the radiator was the hamster's cage.

"We mustn't make any loud noises," Mandy whispered. "Hamsters are easily frightened." She bent down to peer into the cage. It was big and had a raised platform with a ladder leading up to it. There was a wheel for Frisky to exercise on and a gnawing block for him to sharpen his teeth. Frisky was inside a wooden box on top of the platform. His little face was peeping out of a nest of soft hay.

Mandy drew in her breath. "Oh, look, James! Isn't he sweet?"

Frisky gazed out at her with jet black, shiny eyes. His nose twitched and his whiskers wiggled.

"He's gorgeous," James said in a hushed voice. "Will he come out, do you think?"

"We might have to wait until it starts to get dark," Mandy said. She knew hamsters usually slept in the daytime.

But as Mandy spoke, Frisky suddenly pushed his way through the hay and popped out on to his platform. He sat up on his hind legs and began washing his face. His paws had four fingers. His little body was round and plump and his fur was brownish-grey.

Mandy was enchanted. She put her finger through the bars of the cage and wiggled it.

"He's very tiny." James peered closer.

"Dad told me he's a Russian hamster," Mandy said. "He said they're much smaller than the golden hamsters that most people have."

"What's that in the corner of the cage?" James pointed to a place where it looked as if Frisky had piled the sawdust up in a heap.

"That must be his food store," Mandy said.

"Food store?" James said, looking puzzled.

"Yes," said Mandy. "Hamsters always make a food store. In the wild they live in the desert so they never know where their next meal's coming from. With a food store they can eat whenever they like."

"I see," said James. "What a good idea."

"You seem to know a lot about it, Mandy." Grandad's voice came from the doorway.

Mandy turned, her eyes shining. "Mum gave me one of those leaflets they keep in the surgery. You know, the ones that tell you all about your pet and how to take care of it properly."

"Oh, yes." Grandad bent down to peer at Frisky. "What do you think of the little fellow, then?"

"He's great," said Mandy and James together. They laughed.

"Can we take him out and play with him?" asked James.

"I think we'd better let him settle down first," Grandad said. "Come and see him again tomorrow. I'm sure he'll be used to his holiday home by then."

There was a bag of hamster mix on the

10

floor beside the table. It was made up of seeds and cereal flakes and dried fruit. There was also a bag of wood shavings for the bottom of Frisky's cage and a bundle of hay for his nest-box.

"Maybe he should have a few more toys," Mandy said to Grandad and James when they had said goodbye to Frisky and were on their way down the stairs. "Hamsters get bored very easily."

"You're the expert," Grandad said. He went to put the kettle on to make a cup of tea.

Gran was still clattering away in her study.

"Tea, Dorothy!" Grandad called. "Want some lemonade, you two?"

"Yes, please," they both said.

Mandy was looking thoughtful. "I'll bring Frisky a tube tomorrow," she said. "You know, one of those from the inside of a kitchen roll."

"What for?" asked James.

"For him to run in and out of," Mandy said. She sat down at the table. "Oh, Grandad, I can't wait to play with him."

Gran came in for her cup of tea.

"Frisky has been asleep since Mary brought him over," she said. "So I haven't had a proper look at him yet."

"Well, he's awake now, Gran, and you can take it from me," Mandy's eyes shone, "he's just gorgeous!"

2

Gran's good idea

When Gran had finished her tea, Mandy and James took her to see Frisky. As they went into the spare bedroom they heard a squeaking noise.

Frisky was fully awake and was inside his exercise wheel, running as fast as he could. The wheel was whizzing round so fast that it was almost a blur. Then Frisky dived out and ran up and down his ladder as fast as he could go.

James and Mandy burst out laughing.

Gran was peering into the cage. "Well, I never," she said, looking amazed.

Frisky stopped dashing round his cage and sat on his hind legs to gnaw a sunflower seed.

"I'll bring him a bit of carrot tomorrow," Mandy said. "And a piece of apple."

"Apple *and* carrot?" Gran laughed.

"Yes," Mandy said. "And celery and lettuce. Hamsters need things like that to keep them healthy."

Gran was still peering at Frisky. "He looks a bit like a mouse to me." She didn't sound sure whether she liked him or not.

"I suppose he does a bit," Mandy said.

"But a nice mouse," James said.

Gran gave a little shiver. "You might think mice are nice, James," she said. "But I don't think I do."

Mandy chuckled. "Well, Frisky's lovely anyway, don't you think?"

Gran still didn't look very sure. "I'll get

used to him, I expect," she said.

"We could help you look after him if you like," Mandy said. "Couldn't we, James?"

"We certainly could," James said.

"That would be lovely," said Gran.

"And Grandad says we can play with him when he's settled down," Mandy said. "We'll come tomorrow if that's OK?"

"Fine with me," Gran said. "I've got a busy week ahead so I'd be grateful if you'd keep Frisky amused."

"We will!" they both said at once.

They said goodbye to Gran and Grandad and made their way home. It was getting dark by now and a grey mist was settling over the village green.

"Bye, James," Mandy said as they parted at James's gate. "I'll call for you in the morning."

Mandy felt happy as she ran off towards Animal Ark. Helping Gran and Grandad look after Frisky would be almost like having a hamster of her own.

A white van with TONY BROWN, PAINTER AND DECORATOR written in big letters on the side stood outside the gate of Animal Ark. The surgery and the house were getting a new coat of paint.

Mandy ran down the brick path and burst in through the door. "Mum! Mum! Where are you?"

"Here, Mandy," Mrs Hope called from the examining room. Mandy ran through.

"Oh, Mum, you must go and see Frisky," she said excitedly. "He's so clever and cute! He's got an exercise wheel and he runs round like mad."

Mrs Hope was hunting for something in a box on the floor. Mr Hope was out on a call.

"I'll pop over as soon as I can," Mrs Hope said. "I'm dying to meet him." She frowned. "Now where is that box of dressings? I can't find a thing since that wretched decorator arrived."

Mandy moved aside another cardboard box and perched herself up on the examining table. She'd had to pack up all her toys and books and take down her animal posters because her bedroom was going to be decorated too. "I wish I could have a hamster of my own," she sighed.

"Sorry, Mandy." Mrs Hope was still rummaging about in the box. "You know the rules. We just haven't got time to look after pets."

"Yes, I know." Mandy brightened up. "Never mind, playing with Frisky during the holiday will be almost as good."

Mrs Hope suddenly gave a shout. "Here it is! I knew it was here somewhere." She took out a box of dressings and put it on top of the cabinet. Then she gave Mandy a quick hug. "I'm sure Gran will be grateful for your help. She's really busy this week organising a jumble sale in the village hall."

"Perhaps James and I could help her with that too?" Mandy said.

"I'm sure you could," Mrs Hope said. "It looks as if you're going to have lots to do this holiday then."

"Yep," Mandy said. "Then there's the firework display. James and I promised to help build the bonfire." She frowned. "I hope people will remember to keep their pets in. They get really scared of fireworks."

There was going to be a huge bonfire and firework display in the field behind the high street. Everyone in the village would be going. James's dad was on the organising committee.

"I'll get Jean to put a reminder on the board in the waiting-room," Mrs Hope said. Jean Knox was Animal Ark's receptionist.

"That's a brilliant idea, Mum," Mandy said.

She got down off the couch and went out to the back room. There were several animals out there. In one wire cage, a large white rabbit with pink eyes was nibbling a carrot.

"What's this bunny here for, Mum?" Mandy called. She opened the cage door and gently stroked the rabbit's fur.

Mrs Hope came through. "He's had a infected foot," she explained. "It's much better now so he's going home tomorrow."

A small black cat was asleep in another cage. Mandy went to look. "What about him?" she asked.

"He's a she," Mrs Hope said with a smile. "She's having an operation tomorrow."

"Poor thing." Mandy gazed at the sleeping cat. She always felt very sad at the thought of animals being ill.

"She's not sick," Mrs Hope explained. "She's just having an operation to prevent her having kittens."

One of the cages was covered with a dark cloth. Mandy lifted a corner and peeped in. A creature about the size of a small rabbit was curled up in a ball in one corner. Mandy drew in her breath.

"What's *that*?"

"A chinchilla," Mrs Hope said.

The chinchilla stirred and stretched. Mandy could see it had thick silver-grey fur, long ears and a bushy tail.

"Isn't he lovely!" Mandy said. She thought the chinchilla was one of the prettiest animals she had ever seen.

"Yes," Mrs Hope said. "They're quite unusual, you know."

"When did he come in, Mum?" asked Mandy.

"Yesterday," Mrs Hope said. "He's not at all well, I'm afraid."

"Oh, dear. What's wrong with him?"

"Some kind of lung infection, we think. He's had some medicine and seems to be getting a bit better."

"I'd love to cuddle him." Mandy looked longingly at the little grey creature.

"Maybe when he's better." Mrs Hope glanced at the clock on the wall. "Come on, Mandy. Dad will be in for his tea soon."

Mandy took one last look at the animals

and followed Mrs Hope through into the house.

It wasn't long before Mr Hope walked in. Mandy told him all about Frisky before he had even had time to take his coat off. He laughed when she told him about the exercise wheel.

"Does it squeak?" he asked.

Mandy grinned. "Yes, it does a bit."

"Put a spot of cooking oil on it," Mr Hope said. "That will cure it and it won't do the hamster any harm if he happens to lick it."

"I'll tell Gran," Mandy said.

They had just finished tea when the phone rang.

"I'll answer it." Mandy ran through into the hall.

"Mandy!" It was Gran and she sounded in a bit of a panic.

"What's up?" Mandy asked.

"It's Frisky," Gran said. "There's something wrong with him. Can you get Mum or Dad to come and take a look at him?"

"Oh, yes, of course," Mandy said. "We'll

come straight away." Her stomach turned over. She didn't think she could bear it if Frisky was ill.

She dashed back into the kitchen.

"Mum, Dad," she gasped. "Can you come with me to Gran's? There's something wrong with Frisky."

"Oh dear." Mrs Hope took off her apron. "I'll come. Dad can stay here in case there are any emergency calls. Is that all right, Adam?"

Mr Hope was sitting at the table reading his vet's magazine. "Yes, go ahead. I hope Frisky's all right."

"Oh, so do I," Mandy said.

"We'll take the car," Mrs Hope said when they got outside. "Just in case Frisky needs to come back to the surgery."

Mandy felt sick with worry as she climbed into the car next to her mum. Frisky had been perfectly all right when she and James were at Lilac Cottage earlier on.

They found Gran waiting for them when they arrived. She hurried up the stairs in front of them and thrust open the door to Frisky's room.

"I think he's got mumps," she said anxiously.

Mrs Hope took one look at Frisky and burst out laughing.

"It's not funny, Emily!" Gran sounded indignant. "Look at him!"

Frisky was sitting on top of his nest-box. He gazed at them with beady, bright eyes. His face was huge. His cheeks were puffed out to three times their normal size.

"Oh, Mum!" Mrs Hope laughed and shook her head. "He hasn't got mumps; he's storing food in his cheek pouches!"

"What?" Gran was peering at Frisky with a worried look on her face.

Mrs Hope quickly told Gran that hamsters have large pouches in their cheeks in which to keep food. She pointed to his store in the corner. "They have a food store too, look."

Gran began to laugh too. "Oh, dear," she said, wiping her eyes. "What a silly woman I am." She turned to Mandy. "Honestly, Mandy, I know absolutely nothing about hamsters."

"Never mind, Gran," Mandy said.

"Look," Gran said, "I've got an idea. Why don't you come and stay here for the holidays, Mandy? You could be full time resident hamster-keeper for me." She turned to Mrs Hope. "What do you think, Emily?"

"I think it would be a lovely idea," Mrs Hope said. "It's not much fun at Animal Ark at the moment with ladders and cans of paint all over the place. How about it, Mandy?"

Mandy's eyes were shining. Stay with Gran and look after Frisky for a whole week! It would be fantastic. "Oh, Mum," she said. "Can I really?"

Mrs Hope gave her a hug. "Really," she said. "It will save you popping over here every five minutes."

"Hear that, Frisky?" said Mandy. "I'm going to stay here and look after you."

Frisky gazed at her and twitched his nose.

Mandy looked up at her gran. "He says it's a good idea."

Gran chuckled. "I can see he's going to have the holiday of a lifetime."

"Yes," Mandy said. "And so am I."

3

A spring clean

In the morning Mandy jumped out of bed, dressed quickly and packed a few clothes in her bag. She ran downstairs, ducking under a ladder in the hallway.

Tony Brown was at the top of the ladder painting the ceiling. There were a couple of large paint tins lying open on the floor.

"Morning, Mandy," Tony called as Mandy

sidled past. "Off on your holidays?"

"Yes, I am," Mandy said. She told him where she was going.

"Hamster, eh?" Tony came down the ladder. "Nice things, hamsters. I had one when I was a kid. His name was Lazy."

"Lazy!" Mandy exclaimed. "That's a funny name."

"It wasn't for him," Tony said with a grin. "He slept most of the time."

Mandy laughed. She hoped Frisky wouldn't sleep *all* the time, otherwise she would never get to play with him.

In the kitchen, Mr and Mrs Hope were sitting at the breakfast table.

Mr Hope looked up from his morning paper. "Off to Hamster Hotel then, Mandy?" he said.

"Hamster Hotel!" Mandy laughed. "That's a great name!"

"Frisky's a very lucky little fellow." Mrs Hope got up and put on her white vet's coat. It was almost time for morning surgery. "He'll be the best looked after hamster in Welford, I reckon."

"So do I." Mandy was looking in the bin for the middle of a kitchen roll.

"What are you looking for, Mandy?" her mum asked.

Mandy quickly explained. "Hamsters love running in and out of tunnels," she said.

"There's one in the surgery I think. Come through with me." Mandy followed her mum. "You mustn't give him anything made of soft plastic to play with, you know, Mandy," Mrs Hope said.

"I won't," Mandy said quickly. "He's got very sharp teeth. He'd only bite through it."

"That's right. Plastic wouldn't do his tummy any good at all."

Jean Knox was at her desk opening the day's mail.

"Hello, Jean," Mandy said. "I'm going to be staying at Hamster Hotel for the holiday." She grinned.

"Hamster Hotel?" Jean looked at Mandy over the top of her glasses. "Where on earth's that?"

Mandy told her.

Jean laughed. "Have fun."

* * *

After breakfast, Mandy washed up, then picked up her bag. "Well, Dad," she said, "I'm off now."

Mr Hope kissed her goodbye. "Me too," he said. "I've got to go up to Syke Farm to look at a sick calf. Have a great time, Mandy." He went through to the surgery to get his bag.

On the way to Lilac Cottage Mandy met Walter Pickard walking to the post office. Walter was an old friend of Mandy's grandad. They were both bell-ringers at the village church.

"Where are you off to then, young miss?" Walter asked when he saw Mandy striding along with her bag. He laughed when she told him she was going to Hamster Hotel.

"And I'd better hurry," she said. "It's time for Frisky's breakfast. Oh, don't forget to keep your cats in on Thursday evening, will you, Mr Pickard?"

Mandy was very fond of Walter's three lively cats, Missie, Tom and Scraps.

Walter frowned. "Thursday evening?"

"Yes," Mandy reminded him. "Bonfire night. There will be lots and lots of fireworks."

"Oh, yes, of course," Walter said. "Thanks for reminding me."

Before she went to Lilac Cottage, Mandy called in at James's to tell him the good news.

"Lucky thing. All those yummy cakes," James said. He was very fond of Gran's baking.

Mandy laughed. "Why don't you come over when you've had breakfast?" she said. "We'll clean Frisky out and have a game with him if he's awake."

"Right." James was trying to stop Blackie from hurtling out of the door. "See you later."

At Lilac Cottage, Gran had just finished typing out a notice announcing the jumble sale.

"Ah, Mandy," she said as Mandy came in and dumped her bag on the chair. "Just the person I wanted to see."

"How's Frisky this morning?" Mandy asked.

"I peeped into his room but he must have been asleep."

Mandy felt disappointed. She would have loved to say hello to Frisky but she knew it would be wrong to disturb him. It looked as if she would have to be up very early in the morning to catch him before he dozed off.

"I'm not surprised he was asleep," Gran said. "I could hear him whizzing round on that wheel all night. He's probably tired out."

Mandy told her about Mr Hope's suggestion to stop the wheel squeaking.

"We can oil it when we clean him out," she said.

"Well," Gran said. "When you've done that will you do something for *me*?"

"Course I will, Gran." Mandy took her bag into the hall. She'd unpack her things later.

Gran was still gazing at the notice she had typed out.

GRAND JUMBLE SALE,
VILLAGE HALL, 2PM SATURDAY
IN AID OF CHURCH FUNDS
If you have any jumble please take it to
Lilac Cottage before Friday.

"Do you think this is all right, Mandy?" she asked.

"Looks fine to me," Mandy gazed over Gran's shoulder.

"Right." Gran rolled up the notice.

"Would Jean make some photocopies for me?"

"I'm sure she would," Mandy said.

"And do you think you and James could take them round the village?" Gran asked. "I want as many people to know about the sale as possible."

"OK, Gran," Mandy said. "No problem."

"The vicar might put one on the church notice-board," Gran said thoughtfully.

"Right." Mandy fiddled with her fingers. She was getting impatient to see Frisky. "And I'll ask Jean to put one up at Animal Ark," she said.

"Great," Gran said. "I'm afraid it's a bit short notice. I've been so busy I haven't had time to do them until now." She got up. "Never mind, people usually come up trumps where church funds are concerned."

Mandy was hovering anxiously near the door. "Can I clean Frisky out before I go?"

Gran smiled and gave her a hug. "Of course," she said. "Pets come first!"

Mandy was halfway up the stairs when

there was a knock at the door. She ran back down.

James stood on the doorstep. "I came as quickly as I could," he said. He held up a bag with a carrot and an apple inside. "I've brought Frisky's breakfast."

"Great! Thanks, James. Come on," she said. "We've got a million things to do today."

At first, Frisky was nowhere to be seen. But when Mandy bent to peep into his nest she could just see a hint of grey-brown fur among the soft hay of his bed. There he was, curled up tight as a ball, and fast asleep.

"Is it OK to clean the cage out now?" James asked.

"If we're very careful." Mandy gently unlatched the door of Frisky's cage. "And we shouldn't disturb his food store," she said.

Mandy carefully took out all the old bits of food and wood shavings from the bottom. She put it on some newspaper and wrapped it up. Then she spread out some clean shavings. She put Frisky's toys back in, together with the cardboard roll she had brought from Animal Ark.

Meanwhile, James took Frisky's water bottle and filled it with clean water from the bathroom basin. Frisky's little china food bowl needed filling up, too. James tipped some hamster mix into it then added a piece of apple and carrot.

"Quite a feast," he said.

Mandy smiled. "Hamster Hotel is famous for its good food," she laughed.

Finally, Mandy dabbed a drop of cooking oil on the centre of Frisky's wheel. She spun it round. There wasn't a squeak to be heard.

"There we are," she said when she had finished. "All spick and span."

Frisky had slept through the whole thing. Mandy peered into the nest hopefully. Maybe he would wake up, just for five minutes? But there was no sign of movement. Mandy sighed. They really would have to wait until later to have a game with him.

"Come on," she whispered to James. She picked up the bundle of newspaper. "We'll come back after lunch, shall we? I want to

put some of Gran's posters up round the village."

"Right," James said in a hushed voice.

They tiptoed out of the room and went downstairs.

"What shall I do with this, Gran?" Mandy asked.

Gran eyed the bundle of newspaper. "You can put it on Grandad's compost heap," she said.

"I'll do it." James took the paper from Mandy and went outside. Mandy set off down the path with Gran's jumble sale poster. James soon caught her up and together they made their way towards Animal Ark.

The vicar of Welford, Reverend Hadcroft, was sitting in the waiting-room with a cat basket at his feet. Jean was on the phone.

"Hello, Mr Hadcroft," they said as they came through the door.

"Hello, you two," Mr Hadcroft said.

Mandy sat down beside him. She peered into the basket. "What's wrong with Jemima? I hope she's not sick."

"No, she's due for an injection, that's all."

Mandy felt relieved. She loved the vicar's tabby cat and would have hated her to be ill.

Mrs Hope's head appeared round the surgery door. "Mr Hadcroft?" she called.

Mr Hadcroft picked Jemima's basket up. "See you, Mandy. See you, James."

Jean Knox was still on the phone. She was talking to Mrs Ponsonby about her Pekinese, Pandora.

"Yes, yes," she was saying. "Mr Hope will come as soon as he can."

"Is Pandora ill?" Mandy asked anxiously when Jean put the phone down.

Jean shook her head. "No, just short of breath," she said. "She needs to go on a diet. That woman spoils her dog rotten."

Mandy showed Jean Gran's poster. "Do you mind if I make some copies?"

"Help yourself," Jean said.

"Thanks," said Mandy, and she and James went through to the back room where the photocopier was kept.

"A dozen should be enough," Mandy

said. When they'd finished, she took one through to Jean. "Could you put this up on the board, please, Jean?"

"Will do," Jean said. "Now shoo, you two, I'm very busy."

Mandy and James ran out and made their way down to the post office. Then they worked their way round the village shops. Soon there were posters everywhere.

Mandy hoped Gran's jumble sale would be a great success!

4

Missing!

When Mandy and James got back to Lilac Cottage, Gran was busy sorting out things for the jumble sale. She had filled two black plastic sacks full of old clothes and books. Mandy helped her carry them upstairs.

"About time we got rid of some of this junk," Gran muttered. "Your grandad *will* insist on hoarding things, Mandy.

I'm always telling him off."

Mandy giggled. Grandad *never* threw anything away if he could help it.

"I'm afraid they'll have to go in your room for now, Mandy. There's not really anywhere else to put them." Gran dumped the bags by the cupboard door. "Someone will come round on Friday to pick them up."

Mandy peered hopefully into Frisky's cage. But he was still asleep. The cage was as neat as a new pin. Mandy tried not to be disappointed. She would just have to be patient. There would be plenty of time to play with Frisky that evening.

And when she and James went upstairs after tea there was Frisky, sitting at the bottom of his ladder nibbling a piece of apple.

Mandy drew in her breath. "Isn't he wonderful?" She put her finger through the bars and waggled it. Frisky finished his apple and scampered over to his food bowl. Soon he was gobbling up his hamster mix. Most of it went into his cheek pouches.

"He looks as if he's got mumps again," James laughed. He had heard all about Gran's mistake. "Why don't we take him down to show your gran and grandad?"

Gran was getting ready to go out. There was a meeting of the jumble sale committee and Gran was chairman.

She peered into the cage. "Oh, yes." She still didn't sound too sure. "He is rather sweet after all."

Mandy put the cage on the coffee table in the living-room where Grandad was watching his favourite gardening programme.

Frisky had finished his tea and was running in and out of the cardboard tube.

Grandad peered into the cage. "What a cute little fellow," he said. "Shall we let him out to have a run round?"

Mandy's eyes lit up. It was just what she and James had been waiting for.

"Oh, Grandad, can we?" she said.

Grandad cocked his head to one side. "I think we'd better wait until your Gran's gone, though, don't you? She might not like him running round the living-room."

Gran poked her head round the door. "I'm just off, Tom," she said.

"OK," Grandad waved his hand. "See you later."

They waited until they heard the door bang shut.

"Right," Grandad said. "Coast's clear. Let's make sure there are no holes for him to disappear down first."

James and Mandy searched the room thoroughly.

"No holes!" they said.

"And all the windows are shut," Mandy added.

"I'll put the guard round the hearth." Grandad got up and put the big brass fender in front of the fire. "There, that should be OK."

Mandy was so excited, her heart was beating like a drum as she opened the cage door. She put her hand slowly inside. She picked the hamster up gently and lifted him out.

Frisky sat on the palm of her hand looking at her. "I think he likes me," Mandy said.

"Sensible chap," Grandad chuckled.

Suddenly Frisky turned and ran up Mandy's arm. He sat on her shoulder, then disappeared inside the collar of her sweat-shirt. She sat perfectly still. She could feel Frisky running down her back and round her waist. It tickled so much it was all she could do to stop herself wriggling. Then, suddenly, he appeared on her lap.

"Could I hold him?" James had been watching.

"Of course you can."

Mandy picked Frisky up and passed him to James. He stroked the hamster then put him on his knee. Frisky suddenly ran round James's waist and disappeared.

James sat as still as a stone. "Where's he gone?" He hardly dared breathe.

"I don't know," Mandy said.

Then a lump appeared in the pocket of James's tracksuit top.

Grandad roared with laughter. "He's in your pocket," he said. "The cheeky little blighter."

Suddenly Frisky's nose appeared and he

scampered out of James's pocket, down
the side of the chair and on to the floor.
He ran around, then disappeared under
the sideboard.

Mandy lay flat on the floor. She could see
Frisky sitting on his hind legs by the
skirting-board. He was gazing back at her
with bright, beady eyes.

Suddenly the door opened and Gran
came in.

"Forgot my notebook," she said, heading
for her study.

"Gran!" Mandy gasped. "Shut the . . ."

But it was too late, Frisky had spotted the opening. He dropped down on all fours and scurried out of the room as fast as he could.

"Oh, no," Mandy wailed. "He's gone out!" She dashed into the hall.

Gran looked round. "Who has?"

"Frisky," James said. He ran out after Mandy.

Grandad sat in his chair, chuckling. "He won't go far, Mandy," he called. "Don't worry." Then he suddenly looked serious. "I hope you shut the back door, Dorothy."

"Yes, I did," she said.

"Thank goodness for that," Grandad said.

By now Frisky had completely disappeared. Mandy and James ran all over looking for him.

"Do you think he could have got up the stairs?" James asked.

Mandy shook her head. She felt close to tears. "I don't know," she wailed.

Gran came back out with her notebook. She was walking very carefully, afraid she might step on the escaped hamster.

"You'll have to find him, Mandy." Gran looked serious. "Mary won't be very pleased if she comes back from holiday and he's gone missing."

"I know, Gran. I'm really sorry," Mandy said, close to tears.

Gran put her arm round her. "It was my fault for opening that door."

Mandy shook her head. "No, it wasn't. I shouldn't have let him out. I just wanted to hold him." A tear ran down her cheek.

Gran gave her a quick hug. "Don't worry, Mandy, he's got to be in the house somewhere. If he's still missing I'll help look when I get back." She slipped out of the back door, shutting it quickly behind her.

Mandy and James searched for Frisky until it was time for James to go home.

Mandy's face was glum as she said good-bye to him at the front door.

"I just don't know what we're going to do," she said. She couldn't bear to think of the little creature lost somewhere.

"You could make a trap," James suggested.

Mandy looked at him in horror. "What? Like a mouse-trap?"

"No, silly," James said. "A bottle."

Mandy looked puzzled. "What do you mean?"

"Well," James said. "You get a tall glass jar and put some food and bedding in it."

"Then what?" Mandy asked.

"Then you leave it sideways on the floor. When the hamster goes in to get the food he can't climb out through the neck, it's too slippery."

Mandy's face brightened. "How do you know all this?"

"I read it in a book," James said. He zipped up his coat. "It's supposed to work every time."

"James, you're brilliant!" Mandy cried.

"I know." James laughed as he let himself out through the front door.

Mandy closed the door behind him and sighed. She hoped James was right about the hamster trap. If not, she didn't know *what* they were going to do.

"Any sign of the little chap?" Grandad asked when Mandy got back into the front room.

She shook her head. "No." She went on to tell Grandad about James's idea.

"Right." Grandad turned off the television. "One of those tall jars Gran uses for bottling fruit would be ideal, I reckon. There's a whole shelf of them in the pantry." While Grandad got one down Mandy went upstairs and got some hamster mix and bedding. She took a piece of carrot and apple. If they didn't tempt Frisky then nothing would.

"We'll put it in the living-room," Grandad said. "Let's hope he finds it."

That night Mandy lay awake. She kept imagining all sorts of things that might have happened to Frisky. What if he was stuck somewhere? Maybe he was hiding in a cupboard? She had hunted again before she went to bed but there was no trace of him anywhere.

In the middle of the night Mandy awoke from a restless doze. The moon was shining brightly through the gap in her curtains. Mandy got out of bed and crept down-stairs. It was no good. She *had* to see if Frisky was in the jar.

Mandy tiptoed into the living-room. Gran had drawn back the curtains and the room was bright with moonlight. The jar lay near the fender where Mandy had left it. She let out a sigh of disappointment.

The jar was empty!

5

Never a dull moment

Mandy felt close to tears. Then she suddenly realised the apple and the carrot were gone from the jar. The little bundle of hay began to twitch and all of a sudden out popped Frisky. He ran towards the neck of the jar but kept slipping and sliding backwards. James had been right. Frisky couldn't escape.

"Frisky!" Mandy almost shouted for joy. "Thank goodness!" She scooped up the jar and carried it up to her bedroom. "You naughty boy," she scolded as she climbed the stairs. "Don't you ever frighten me like that again!"

As she went along the landing Gran's bedroom door opened. Gran appeared, looking sleepy-eyed.

"Are you all right, Mandy? I heard you go downstairs."

"Yes, thanks, Gran. I'm fine." She held up the jar. "Look!"

"Well, thank goodness for that," Gran said with a sigh. "Is he all right?"

"He's fine," Mandy said.

"Now perhaps we can get some sleep," Gran said. "Grandad's been tossing and turning ever since we got to bed. Who would have thought such a little creature would cause so much worry?" She waggled her finger at Frisky. "Now you behave yourself, young fellow!" She winked at Mandy then went back into her room and closed the door.

Mandy took Frisky into her room. She gently shook him out of the jar and popped him back into his cage. Frisky ran to his exercise wheel, hopped in and began running. The wheel whizzed round and round. He seemed none the worse for his adventure.

Mandy climbed back into bed and was asleep almost as soon as her head touched the pillow.

Next morning she phoned James to tell him the good news.

"Can I bring Blackie round?" James said when she had told him the story. "We said we'd do some training with him, remember?"

"OK," Mandy said. She smiled to herself. Training Blackie was always great fun, although very rarely successful!

Grandad was just going out to do some work in the garden. He was in a strange mood that morning. Mandy had heard him opening and closing drawers and muttering to himself. Then he had stomped downstairs, grabbed a coat from the hall cupboard and gone out, still mumbling something under his breath.

"Could you take that barrowload of cuttings round to the bonfire later, please, Mandy?" he asked as she stepped outside to see if James and Blackie were coming. "They're quite dry and should burn jolly well."

Just then James and Blackie appeared round the side of the cottage. Blackie had his ball in his mouth. He barged through the gate, almost pulling James over.

"Dad's got some old timber for the bonfire," James panted. "I promised him we'd cart that over too. We'll do some training with Blackie first though, shall we, Mandy?"

"If you like," Mandy said.

Grandad grinned. He had seen them trying to train Blackie before. "Good luck," he said and disappeared into his garden shed.

Gran was just going off to her exercise class. Mandy went with her to the front gate.

"If anyone brings any jumble don't forget it's got to go upstairs," Gran reminded her. "I don't want it cluttering up the hall and front room."

"I won't," Mandy promised. "See you later, Gran." She waved as Gran headed off in the direction of the village hall. Then she turned to James. "What are we going to do with Blackie today?" she asked.

"Retrieving," James said. He tried to get the ball out of Blackie's mouth. Blackie growled playfully and twisted his head from side to side. "Labradors are good at that."

"Leave!" Mandy shook her finger at Blackie.

Blackie stared at her from under his eyelids.

"Leave!" she said again.

"Here, Blackie." James took a dog-biscuit from his pocket. Blackie dropped the ball and gobbled up the biscuit. Mandy dived for it.

"Right," she said. "Here we go."

Mandy and James spent the whole morning trying to get Blackie to bring the

ball back. No matter how hard they tried, Blackie would insist on running off round and round the garden with it.

Grandad thought it was better than a comedy show. "You'll have to put him on a long lead and *make* him bring it back," he called, laughing. He leaned on his spade, watching Blackie running round with Mandy and James chasing him.

"It's no good," James panted. "I give in. Blackie's no good at bringing things back and that's that."

Just then a sleek saloon car pulled up outside. A large lady got out. She was wearing a tweed suit and a black hat. It was Mrs Ponsonby. Pandora the Pekinese was peeping out of the window from her special compartment in the back.

"Mr Hope!" Mrs Ponsonby was round the back of the car in three long strides. "I've brought some things for the sale."

"Oh, good morning, Mrs Ponsonby," Grandad called. He put down his spade and hurried to the gate. "That's very kind of you, thank you very much."

"There's one of darling Pandora's old baskets." Mrs Ponsonby opened the boot. "And some other bits and pieces." She piled the basket and several cardboard boxes into Grandad's arms.

James and Mandy ran to help when they saw Grandad was having a problem balancing all the boxes in his arms. Mandy said hello to Pandora as she passed, then ran to take a box.

Blackie, meanwhile, lay on the grass, the ball clamped firmly between his jaws.

"How's Pandora, Mrs Ponsonby?" Mandy asked.

"She's been a bit poorly," Mrs Ponsonby replied. "But I've kept her in bed for a couple of days and she seems a bit better, aren't you, darling?" she cooed to Pandora.

Mandy peered through the window. "Maybe a long walk would do her good?" she suggested. "Most dogs love walks."

Mrs Ponsonby shook her head. "It would only tire her out, poor lamb," she said.

Pandora was looking at Mandy with her black, boot-button eyes. She gave a yap then yawned. She lay down, sighed and closed her eyes. Mandy smiled. Pandora obviously didn't think much of *that* idea. "Don't forget to keep her in on Thursday evening, will you?" she said.

"Thursday evening?" Mrs Ponsonby looked puzzled.

"The bonfire," Mandy said.

"Oh, yes, of course!" Mrs Ponsonby exclaimed. "Those horrible fireworks. Don't worry, I'll make sure Pandora is tucked up safely in bed."

Mandy smiled again. Pandora certainly was the most spoiled dog around.

She helped Grandad take the stuff upstairs.

"Someone else is here with some jumble," James called as they went back out into the garden.

"Phew." Grandad took off his cap and wiped his brow. "*When* am I going to get my gardening done?"

By the time Thursday came there was a great pile of jumble in Mandy's room. In fact there was so much that it had spilled out on to the landing. Boxes of books and bric-a-brac, old toys, clothes and all kinds of other things.

"Gran will be pleased," Mandy said as she helped Grandad cart yet another load up the stairs.

"She certainly will," Grandad said. "Everyone's gone mad, I reckon. Some of this stuff is as good as new."

Mandy smiled to herself. She thought of Grandad's favourite old gardening jumper. He always said *that* was as good as new even though it was full of holes. Gran was always telling him he should throw it away.

Every day Mandy and James made sure Frisky's cage was spick and span and he had plenty of fresh food and water.

Frisky usually woke up about teatime. His antics kept Mandy and James in fits. There was certainly never a dull moment when Frisky was awake. And they were very careful never to let him escape again.

By now, the bonfire in the field behind the village high street looked like a mountain. When they weren't looking after Frisky or taking Blackie for walks, Mandy and James helped to build it.

"I hope they're going to make sure no hedgehogs have crawled under it," Mandy said to James as they tipped yet another barrowload of Grandad's garden cuttings on to the heap.

"Dad built a platform first," James assured her. "That means they should be able to see if there are any underneath before they light it."

"Brilliant," Mandy said. She grabbed the empty barrow and ran on ahead. "I can't wait for tonight."

The bonfire was to be lit at six o'clock. Mandy made sure Frisky had enough food and water for the evening then put on her coat and boots.

Outside it was a chilly, misty evening. People were already making their way along the high street towards the field where the bonfire stood.

Mandy walked between Gran and Grandad. Her mum and dad were waiting for them outside Animal Ark. They were meeting James and Mrs Hunter at the bonfire. Mr Hunter had gone earlier to make sure the firework display was ready.

"While I think of it, Mandy," her mum said as they strolled past the post office and down the narrow alley that led to the bonfire field, "would you like to come shopping in Walton tomorrow?"

"That would be great," Mandy said. "I bet James would like to come too. I'll ask him." Her eyes lit up as she suddenly had an idea. "I could get Frisky a present to remind him of his holiday at Hamster Hotel!"

Mrs Hope smiled. "How's he getting on?"

"He's fine," Mandy said. She tried not to think about how much she would miss Frisky when Mary came to collect him.

A large crowd had gathered round the bonfire. Almost everyone in the village had turned up.

Mandy ran off to find James. He was standing behind the ropes watching his dad getting ready to light the huge bonfire.

There was a stall nearby selling hot dogs and hot baked potatoes and the smell made Mandy's stomach rumble.

She asked James if he would like to go shopping the following day. "I'm going to get Frisky a present," she told him.

"That sounds great!" James jumped up and down to try to keep warm. "Maybe we could buy a really good one between us?"

"Let's go and see your dad." Mandy scrambled under the rope and ran over to Mr Hunter. James followed.

"Have you checked for hedgehogs?" Mandy asked anxiously.

Mr Hunter nodded. "There weren't any," he said. "Now get back behind the ropes, please, you two," he added. "It's not safe here."

When Mandy and James rejoined the crowd, Mr Hunter lit the taper and there was a shout as the bonfire caught and roared. The orange flames lit up the night sky. Everyone clapped.

Then, with a bang and a shower of sparks, the firework display began.

Even though she was enjoying herself, Mandy couldn't help worrying about the village pets.

"I do hope everyone remembered to keep their dogs and cats in," she said in James's ear after a very loud bang that echoed around the field like thunder.

"Well, Blackie and Benji are tucked up safe and sound," James said.

Mandy suddenly decided she couldn't resist the smell of the hot dogs any longer.

"Do you want a hot dog, James?"

"Mmm," James licked his lips. "Yes, please."

They wandered over to the stall where Mr Oliver was dishing out the food.

Mandy had just finished eating when she spotted a dark shadow by the hedge. She clutched James's arm.

"James, look! What's that over there?"

James peered into the shadows. "Where?"

Mandy pointed. She couldn't believe her eyes. A small black dog was creeping along the edge of the field.

"There!" she cried. "Come on, James, quick!" Mandy ran across, James right behind her.

By now, the little creature was crouched by the gatepost, hunched up, its tail between its legs. It was trembling with fright. It flinched as a rocket took off and exploded in a blizzard of stars.

Just as it was about to dash off into the road, Mandy grabbed it. The dog was freezing cold and whimpering with fear. Mandy crouched down and scooped him up into her arms. She noticed he was wearing a collar with a silver disc attached to it.

"Oh, James, he's terrified." She stroked the dog's head. How could anyone be so cruel as to let their dog out on a night like this?

"Poor thing," Mandy was murmuring. "Come on, James, let's get him away from the noise."

Cradling the dog against her coat Mandy strode through the gate.

"Where are you taking him?" James hurried after her.

"Back to Animal Ark," she said. "He'll be safe there."

Gran and Grandad were talking to Walter Pickard. Mandy waited while James ran to tell them where they were going. Then they headed off across the village green towards Animal Ark. The dog was trembling and making little whining noises.

"Don't worry," Mandy soothed. "You're safe now." She unzipped her jacket and put it round him. The sooner they got the little dog into the warmth of Animal Ark, the better.

6

A present for Frisky

Indoors, Mandy got a blanket and wrapped it round the little dog. She sat by the fire, hugging him on her lap. James bent down to stroke his head. The dog had stopped shaking and had nestled as close to Mandy as he could.

"Here," Mandy said to James. "You hold him while I heat up some milk. It'll warm his

tummy up and make him feel much better."

A few minutes later Mandy poured the milk carefully into a small bowl. James put the dog down on the floor. He wobbled a bit then sniffed the milk. Soon he began to lap it up. Mandy kneeled beside him.

"I wonder why his owners didn't shut him in," she said. "They should have known how scared he'd be."

"Have a look on his collar," James said. "It should tell us where he lives."

Mandy turned over the silver disc. "His

name's Bobby," she said. "And there's just a phone number. Welford 876597." She stood up. "I'd better give them a ring. They'll probably be worried about him."

Just then the door opened and Mr Hope came hurrying in. He had come as soon as he heard what had happened. "Gran told me you were here." He bent down. "Is he all right?"

The little dog had finished the milk. He sat huddled up close to the fire. He was licking his chops and looking at Mr Hope with wide, scared eyes.

Mr Hope held his head and looked into his eyes. He ran his hand down his back and legs. "He seems OK now."

Mandy gave the little mongrel a hug. "His name's Bobby," Mandy said. "I was just going to ring his owners."

She went out into the hall to use the phone. A minute or two later, she came back. "He comes from those houses behind the church," she said. "I said we'd take him home."

"Did they know he was out?" James asked.

"Yes. They were really worried. He

belongs to their little girl and she's been crying all evening. They said they had been looking everywhere for him. He's always running away."

"Well, this might have taught him a lesson," Mr Hope said. "Although it's really up to the owners to keep their dogs under control."

Mr Hope went to get a spare dog lead he kept in the surgery. When he came back Mandy and James were ready to go.

"Gran and Grandad have gone home," Mr Hope told her. "I'll give them a ring to tell them you're on your way back."

"Thanks," Mandy said.

"We missed the rest of the fireworks," James remarked as they hurried along the main street towards the church.

"Never mind," Mandy said. "I would rather have been helping Bobby."

"Me too," James agreed.

They found Bobby's house and knocked at the door. A little girl answered it. Her eyes were red and she looked very unhappy. Her face lit up though, when she saw Mandy and James standing on the doorstep with Bobby.

When he saw her, Bobby's tail began wagging nineteen to the dozen. He gave a little whine and began jumping up at her.

The little girl burst into tears and bent down to pick him up.

"Oh, Bobby, you naughty boy!" she sobbed, burying her face in the soft fur of his neck.

Bobby began whining and licking her face.

"Oh, Bobby," she said again.

Mandy felt like crying too. Bobby's owner had obviously been frantic.

"My dad says he's all right," Mandy said. "But he's had a very lucky escape," she added gently. "You'll have to keep a close eye on him from now on."

"We will, I promise." The girl wiped her eyes. "Thank you very much."

They could hear her still talking to Bobby as she turned back into the house and closed the door.

When Mandy had said goodbye to James and got back to Lilac Cottage, Gran had a steaming cup of hot chocolate ready for her.

"How did you get on?" she asked as

Mandy came in. "Poor little dog."

"OK," Mandy said. She told her gran about the little girl.

"I bet you told her off," Grandad said when he came in. He knew how angry Mandy got if she thought animals were not being looked after properly.

"No, I didn't," Mandy said. "She was too upset."

Grandad gave Mandy a hug. "Bobby was a very lucky dog if you ask me," he said.

Mandy finished her drink and ran upstairs to see Frisky. He was dashing round and round the cage, up his ladder, through his cardboard tunnel and in and out of his exercise wheel. The wheel was squeaking badly again. Cooking oil didn't seem to last very long.

Mandy decided Frisky was quite the most charming pet she had ever *almost* had, even though she sometimes felt quite tired just watching him!

She sat by his cage and told Frisky about the night's adventures. He seemed to listen to every word she was saying. Then she took him out and let him have a little run around. She picked him up and he sat on her hand. Then he darted up her sleeve, sat on her collar for a moment and disappeared down her neck.

Mandy chuckled. She was quite used to the feeling of Frisky running about inside her clothes by now. When he popped out of her sleeve again she caught him and put him carefully back into his cage.

She sighed. She was really going to miss Frisky when it was time for him to go home.

The following morning Mrs Hope picked up Mandy and James to take them shopping. Before they set off, she paid a visit to Frisky. He was very sleepy and almost ready for his daytime snooze.

"He's really sweet," Mrs Hope said. "And very clean and healthy. You're doing a grand job, you two."

On the way to Walton, Mandy gazed out of the window at the passing fields and trees. The mist of the early morning had given way to bright sunshine. Tomorrow she would be busy helping with the jumble sale and the next day Frisky would be going home and she would be going back to Animal Ark. The week seemed to have flashed by.

"What are we going to get Frisky?" James asked.

Mandy was thoughtful. "I'm not sure. We'll have to look and see what they've got in the pet shop."

"He's already got a wheel, a tube and a gnawing block," James said.

Mrs Hope laughed. "Well, what *do* you buy the hamster who's got everything?"

"A friend?" James suggested.

Mandy shook her head. "No, hamsters have to live on their own. They fight if you put two together."

Mrs Hope came up with an idea. "You could make him an adventure playground," she suggested.

"Adventure playground?" Mandy said.

"Yes, you could put a small branch into the cage and put little ladders up one side and down the other. Grandad would find you something suitable and you could get the ladders in Walton."

"What a great idea, Mum! We could make it when we get back."

There was a pet shop in Walton where they found just the ladders they wanted. They were made of metal and had hooks at the end.

"We can hook them over the branch," Mandy said. "He's going to love it, I know."

"Then we could hang something to one end of the branch," James suggested.

"What sort of thing?" Mandy asked.

"How about a couple of wooden cotton reels?" Mrs Hope suggested. "They make great hamster toys."

Mandy and James bought one ladder each. Then they bought a new gnawing block as Frisky had almost bitten his way through his old one. It was important for hamsters to keep their teeth short. Last of all, they bought a bag of special luxury hamster mix.

On the way home, they sat in the back of the car making plans.

"We can set the adventure playground up in Frisky's cage while he's asleep," said Mandy.

"Then it will be a surprise when he wakes

up," James said excitedly. "I just can't wait to see what he does!"

"Neither can I," Mandy chuckled.

When they got back to Lilac Cottage, Grandad was outside cleaning the windows. Mandy told him about Frisky's surprise and asked if he would help them.

"Oh, I should think so." Grandad put down his polishing cloth. "Follow me."

He strode off down the path. "I've had a really busy morning," he told them as they went down to the bottom of the garden. "First the car wouldn't start when Gran wanted to go shopping. Then just as I got *that* sorted, John Jenkins came to pick up the jumble. Ah . . ."

He stopped under one of the apple-trees that grew by the fence. "An apple twig," he said. He took out his penknife and cut one off. "Just the job for a hamster's adventure playground. What do you think?"

Mandy took it from him. "Great. Thanks, Grandad."

She suddenly thought of something else. "Do you think Gran would mind if we looked in her sewing box?"

"What for?" Grandad asked.

"A couple of empty wooden cotton reels," James said. "We're going to hang them from the branch."

"I'm sure she won't mind," Grandad said. "Make sure you put everything back, though."

"We will." Mandy and James dashed indoors.

Mandy found two suitable cotton reels while James found some string in a kitchen drawer. Together they tied them on to the apple twig.

Mandy sat back. "Frisky's going to have great fun with those," she said. "Come on, let's set it up while he's still asleep."

They took everything upstairs. Mandy put her finger to her lips. "Let's be very quiet," she whispered.

She opened the door softly. Then she froze with shock. The table by the radiator was empty. It wasn't only the stuff for the jumble sale that had gone.

Frisky had gone too!

7

All locked up

Mandy and James stood gazing at the empty table. They could hardly believe Frisky had just vanished into thin air.

Then Mandy gave a little laugh of relief. "Gran must have moved him," she said. "She knew Mr Jenkins was coming this morning. Maybe she's put Frisky in the living-room."

They ran downstairs. Frisky *wasn't* in the living-room. They looked in the study, then over the rest of the house. Frisky was nowhere to be found.

"Let's go and ask your grandad," James said.

They dashed outside.

"Grandad, where's Frisky?" she called anxiously.

"Frisky? In your room, isn't he?" Grandad had finished cleaning the windows and was in his potting shed.

Mandy shook her head. "No, he's gone."

Grandad tipped his cap to the back of his head and frowned. "Come on, let's have a look."

Mandy and James followed him indoors and back upstairs. "He's not there, honestly," Mandy wailed.

"We've looked *everywhere*," James added.

Grandad stood in the bedroom doorway, his hands on his hips. "Well, I don't know, I'm sure . . ."

Mandy was beginning to feel desperate. Where *could* Frisky have gone?

Then James had an idea.

"Maybe he went with the jumble," he said.

Mandy looked at him in horror. "Surely no one would think we were giving Frisky to a jumble sale," she said.

James shrugged. "If he was asleep in his nest Mr Jenkins wouldn't have been able to see him, would he?"

Grandad looked thoughtful. "You know, James is right," he said. "John might have thought it was an empty cage."

"Oh, Grandad!" Mandy could hardly hold back the tears.

"Come on," Grandad said. He put his arm round her. "Let's give John a ring."

They went back down the stairs. Grandad dialled Mr Jenkins's number but there was no reply.

"Can't we go to his house?" Mandy asked anxiously. "He might just be out in the garden and not able to hear the phone."

Grandad shook his head. "I'm sorry, Mandy, I don't know where he lives. We'll have to wait until your gran gets back from the supermarket. She'll know."

"He wouldn't have taken the jumble to his house though, would he?" James piped up.

Mandy stared at him. Then her face cleared. "No, of *course* he wouldn't!" she said. "He would have taken it to the village hall. Let's go and see." She rushed off to get her coat.

"But it'll be all locked up," Grandad called as they ran out. "You should wait till Gran gets back."

"We'll go and see anyway," Mandy shouted, halfway down the path. "It won't do any harm."

She couldn't possibly wait until Gran got back. She might be ages. She had to do something *now*.

Mandy and James raced down the high street across the green to the village hall. Jean Knox was just coming out of the post office.

"What's the rush, Mandy?" she called.

Mandy skidded to a halt and quickly told Jean what had happened.

"Oh, dear," Jean said. "I hope you find him all right. Let me know if I can help."

"We will!" James called as they rushed off.

Mr Hadcroft was pinning a notice on the church notice-board. Mandy was in such a hurry she nearly ran into him.

"Hey, hey . . . !" He took hold of her arms. "Where's the fire?"

"We've lost Frisky," Mandy panted. She went on to tell him the story.

Mr Hadcroft patted her shoulder. "Well, try not to worry, Mandy, I'm sure he'll be OK."

"I do hope so." Mandy still felt close to tears.

"If I see John Jenkins, I'll tell him," Mr Hadcroft called.

"Thanks," Mandy shouted over her shoulder.

They reached the village hall and hurried through the gate and up the steps. Mandy grabbed the door handle. She twisted and pushed. Nothing happened. Grandad had been right. The hall was all locked up.

James jumped up and down, trying to see

through one of the windows. "I can't reach," he panted.

"Here," Mandy tried to lift him up but he kept slipping out of her grasp.

"It's no good," she panted. "You're too heavy. Can't we find something to stand on?" She looked round desperately.

There was an orange plastic milk crate by the back door. Mandy went to fetch it. She turned it upside down and stood on it.

"I still can't see," she wailed. She was standing on tiptoe and the crate was wobbling like mad.

"You'll fall off," James warned.

Mandy got down. She sat on the crate and put her head in her hands. "Oh, James; poor Frisky. What are we going to do?"

James sat beside her. "Maybe we should go back home and wait for your gran."

"I'm not budging until I find out if he's in there!" Mandy said stubbornly.

James sighed. "OK, but I don't know what good it will do."

Luckily it wasn't long before they spotted Gran's car coming along the road.

Mandy jumped to her feet. "Gran!" She ran to the kerb and waved her arms. "Gran! Gran! Stop!"

Gran pulled up beside her. She wound down the window. "Mandy, what's wrong?" she asked anxiously.

Mandy's words all seemed to tumble over one another as she told Gran what had happened.

"Oh dear." Gran gave a little chuckle. "Poor Frisky. Hop in, you two, I'll take you to John Jenkins's house. He's bound to have a key." When she saw Mandy's worried face she stopped smiling. "Don't worry, Mandy, I'm sure Frisky will be all right."

"That's what everyone keeps saying," Mandy wailed. "But it will be cold and draughty in the hall and he'll be scared stiff if he wakes up in a strange place."

Gran patted her knee. "We'll soon sort this out, don't worry. And he'll be quite safe in his cage, you know."

When they reached Mr Jenkins's house Gran knocked at the door but there was still no answer and the windows were all in darkness.

Mandy jiggled about in her seat. "Oh, James," she said. "What on earth are we going to do now?"

8

Safe and sound

Gran came back to the car looking thoughtful.
She got in and started the engine.

"We'll have to go and get the key from
Mr Markham," she said.

"Who's he?" James asked as they drove
back towards the village centre.

"Chairman of the parish council," Gran
told them. "I know he's got a key to the

hall. I have to collect it from him before our WI meetings."

"I hope *he's* in," Mandy said. "Otherwise I don't know what we're going to do."

They drew up outside Number 2, The Terrace, the home of Mr Markham.

"You two stay here in the warm," Gran said. "I'll go and see."

Mandy peered out of the car window anxiously. It was getting dark now and a cold wind was blowing. There wouldn't be any heating in the village hall. She felt sick with fear. If Frisky was in there it would be much too cold for him.

It wasn't long before someone answered the door. Gran disappeared inside for a minute or two then came back out waving a key. She hurried down the path and got into the car.

"Here we are," she said briskly. She gave the key to Mandy. "Problem solved."

Gran drove quickly along the main street to the village hall. She pulled up outside and Mandy and James jumped out. Mandy unlocked the door and ran inside.

Quickly she clicked on the light. The jumble *was* here. Piles of it. Bags, boxes, even suitcases full of old clothes, all waiting to be sorted out the following morning. Someone had already put up long trestle-tables.

Mandy gave a shiver. It felt freezing, just as she had feared it would be. Frisky would be cold and frightened and so bewildered he wouldn't know *where* he was.

But where *was* Frisky? Mandy and James carefully pulled aside bags and boxes but there wasn't a hamster cage of any description anywhere.

Mandy sat on a chair and burst into tears.

"Don't cry, Mandy," James said. "He's got to be somewhere."

Gran joined them and put her arm round Mandy.

"Don't upset yourself, darling. John must have spotted him and taken him home," Gran said.

"But John's not *at* home," Mandy sobbed.

Gran got up. "We'll return Mr Markham's key, then we'll go and see if John's back."

But when they reached Mr Jenkins's house, it was still in total darkness.

"I'll pop next door," Gran said. "They might know how long he'll be."

When she came back she shook her head. "Sorry, Mandy, he won't be back until late. I'm afraid we'll just have to wait until the morning."

They dropped James off at his gate.

"I'll come round early and see what's happened," he said.

"OK." Mandy sat sadly in the back of the car. She didn't know *how* she was going to get any sleep that night. She would be worrying about Frisky all the time.

When they got home, Grandad was waiting anxiously.

"Any luck?" he asked as they came in.

Gran shook her head. "No, I'm afraid not."

Grandad put his arm round Mandy. "Try not to worry, love," he said. "He's got a snug nest and plenty of food. He'll be all right."

It seemed really quiet in Mandy's room with no hamster whizzing round on his wheel or tearing in and out of his cardboard roll. His adventure playground still lay on the table where Mandy and James had left it.

About ten o'clock Mandy heard the phone ring and Gran's voice answering it. Then Gran came up the stairs. The bedroom door opened.

"Are you asleep, Mandy?"

"No, Gran," she said. "What's up?"

"John Jenkins has just phoned," Gran told her.

Mandy sat up quickly. Her heart thudded. "What did he say?" she asked anxiously.

Gran sat on the bed. "It seems the whole village has found out about Frisky," she said with a smile. "Jean saw Walter in the Fox and Goose. Walter told Mr Hadcroft who said he knew already. Mr Hadcroft phoned Mr Markham who had just got home. Mr Markham phoned John and John phoned me." Gran chuckled. "Quite a jungle telegraph."

Mandy wrung her hands together. "But, Gran, what about *Frisky*?"

"John's got him at home," Gran said with

a smile. "He's absolutely fine."

"Oh, thank goodness!" Mandy threw her arms round her gran's neck in delight.

Gran laughed. "Hey, you're strangling me."

Mandy let go. "Sorry, Gran." Her eyes were shining. "Tell me what happened."

"Wait and see John in the morning," Gran said. "He's taking Frisky to the hall first thing. I said you and James would go and help them sort out the jumble. John can tell you the story himself then."

9

None the worse

The next morning James turned up bright and early. Mandy was still having breakfast.

"Sit down and have some toast and home-made jam," Gran said to James when he arrived. "I'll make you a hot chocolate."

"Thanks, Mrs Hope." James sat down next to Mandy. "Have you had any news about Frisky?" he asked anxiously. "I've been thinking about him all night."

Mandy quickly told him about John's late-night phone call.

"Thank goodness!" James heaped a spoonful of strawberry jam on to his toast. "I hardly slept a wink."

"Are you coming to help sort out the jumble, Tom?" Gran asked Grandad.

Grandad looked up from his gardening magazine. "If you want me to, Dorothy."

"The more the merrier." Gran began clearing away the dishes. Mandy got up to give her a hand but she was in such a hurry she almost dropped a plate. Gran took it from her.

"I can see you're dying to get down to that hall, love," she said. "Off you go, both of you. We'll come along a bit later."

James snatched up the last of his toast and they set off.

"You've got jam all round your mouth." Mandy grinned at James as they hurried along to the hall. She felt on top of the world now she knew Frisky was safe and sound. She just couldn't wait to see him again.

James licked round his mouth. He screwed up his nose and looked at Mandy. "Has it gone?"

"Yep." Mandy grinned. "Race you!" They took off down the street, shouting noisily.

When they got there, the hall was a hive of activity. Half a dozen ladies were sorting out old clothes, a teenage girl was in charge of the tapes and CDs and Mr Hadcroft was arranging a pile of toys.

There was a woman folding up pairs of trousers and putting them in a pile on the table by the door.

"Can we see Mr Jenkins, please?" Mandy panted. She had arrived just seconds before James.

"He's over by the stage." The woman pointed. "Sorting out the garden tools."

A tall man in a flat cap and tweed jacket was tying a bundle of rather battered-looking tools together. As Mandy went up to him, something caught her eye. There, on top of the piano, was Frisky's cage.

Mandy gave a shout and leaped up on the stage. "Frisky!" She had thought he

would be fast asleep but all the hustle and bustle must have woken him up. He was sitting by his food bowl.

Mandy beamed at him through the bars of the cage. "Oh, Frisky, I'm so pleased to see you! Are you all right?"

Frisky twitched his nose then went on eating. He looked perfectly well; perky as anything and stuffing his cheek pouches full of food. He seemed none the worse for his journey round Welford.

"He's fine," a deep voice said from behind her. "You must be Mandy?"

Mandy turned to see Mr Jenkins smiling at her.

"Oh, Mr Jenkins," said Mandy. "I've been so worried about him."

"I know," Mr Jenkins said. "I'm really sorry. When I picked up the jumble I thought the cage was empty."

"I thought that's what had happened." James put his finger through the bars to tickle Frisky under the chin.

"People give all sorts of things to jumble sales. I just thought maybe someone had lost a hamster and was giving away the cage."

"It doesn't matter," Mandy said. "He's safe and sound, that's the main thing."

"When did you find him?" James asked.

"I'd unloaded all the stuff," Mr Jenkins told them, "and was just going to lock up when I heard a strange noise. I'll tell you, it gave me quite a scare."

Mandy frowned. "What do you mean?"

"Well," Mr Jenkins raised his eyebrows. "It was a squeak, squeak . . . I thought it was a ghost!"

Mandy and James burst out laughing.

Mr Jenkins was laughing too.

"What did you do?" Mandy asked.

"Well, I tracked the noise down to a pile of old curtains," Mr Jenkins said. "Then, when I moved them aside, there was the hamster cage with this little chap running inside his wheel like a maniac. I was mighty relieved, I can tell you."

"I bet," James said.

"I was going to phone your gran," Mr Jenkins said. "But I'd promised my wife I'd take her to the pictures in Walton and she was ready when I got back. I'm sorry you were so worried, Mandy."

"It's OK," Mandy beamed him a smile. "As long as he's all right. He's not mine, you see. I've been looking after him for Gran's friend. He's been staying at Hamster Hotel."

It was Mr Jenkins's turn to look surprised. "Hamster Hotel?"

James chuckled. "Lilac Cottage," he explained.

"Oh," said Mr Jenkins. "I see." He looked a bit puzzled and Mandy didn't really think he saw at all.

Gran and Grandad arrived. They came to see Frisky, then went off to help sort out the jumble.

"Do you want to give me a hand?" Gran asked Mandy. "You could help Grandad with the books and magazines if you like, James."

"Right," James said.

"If there's one on dog training, you'd better buy it, James," Mandy called as she went to help Gran.

"Good idea." James began hunting through the pile.

Gran was sorting out a heap of old jumpers and cardigans.

"Hey," Mandy picked one up. "This looks like Grandad's old—"

But she got no further. Gran had snatched the jumper from her fingers. "Shh. He doesn't know," she whispered.

But it was too late. Grandad had seen it. He came rushing over faster than Mandy had ever seen him move before.

"Dorothy!" His voice was like thunder.

Gran was holding the jumper behind her back. "Yes, dear?" she said calmly.

"Dorothy!" Grandad was dodging about, trying to see behind her back. "That looks like . . ."

Everyone had stopped work and was watching.

"It is, Mr Hope," James called. "It's your gardening jumper." Then his hand flew to his mouth. He had given the game away.

Grandad held out his hand towards Gran. "Thank you, James. I'm glad us men stick

together. Give it to me, Dorothy," he ordered sternly.

"It's full of holes," Gran said.

"I like them." Grandad was still holding out his hand.

"It's faded," Gran said.

"I like it faded." Grandad tried to grab the jumper.

"It . . . it . . . smells!" Gran backed away.

"I'll wash it," Grandad promised. "Anyway, it's a nice smell. Earthy . . ."

"It's, it's . . ." Gran couldn't think of anything else.

". . . it's Grandad's favourite jumper," Mandy finished for her.

"Oh, well, all right." Gran gave it to Grandad with a sigh. Everyone laughed and clapped.

Then Gran laughed too. She put her arms round Grandad and gave him a hug. "Oh, Tom, you'll be the death of me," she said wiping her eyes.

"Nonsense." Grandad gave her a loud kiss on the cheek.

"I've been hunting for my jumper everywhere," Grandad said to Mandy when Gran had gone back to sorting jumble. "I might have known your gran would try to pull a trick like that."

Mandy suddenly remembered how Grandad had spent ages looking through all the drawers and cupboards. So that's what he had been up to. She laughed and gave him a hug.

"Is it all right if we take Frisky home, now?" Mandy asked Grandad when all the jumble was sorted neatly into piles on the tables. It was almost lunch-time.

Grandad looked at his watch. "Yes, I'll run you home if you like. We don't want Frisky out in that cold air. We'll come back later for the sale." He glanced over to where Gran was talking to two of the ladies. "Who knows, I might even find myself another jumper with holes in."

Mandy and James chuckled. They said goodbye to everyone and put Frisky carefully in the car. Frisky hadn't been at all worried by the noise and bustle and had gone into his nest for a snooze.

Mandy felt excited as they travelled back to Lilac Cottage.

She just couldn't wait to show Frisky his adventure playground!

10

Farewell

On the way home they passed Mr Hope coming out of Animal Ark.

"Please stop, Grandad," Mandy said. "I *must* tell Dad about Frisky."

Grandad pulled up and she wound down her window.

Mr Hope laughed as he listened to her story.

"I don't know, Mandy," he said. "You do get into some scrapes."

"It wasn't *my* fault," Mandy said indignantly. "We've given Frisky the best care in the world."

"I know, Mandy," her dad said. "Well, we'll be pleased to see you back home. It's been really quiet without you," he added, teasing her.

"Is my bedroom finished?" Mandy asked. She had been looking forward to seeing it now it had been decorated.

"Yep." Mr Hope opened the boot of his car and put his bag inside. "It looks great. Lovely colour, although I expect you'll soon have all your posters up again and we won't be able to see much of the walls."

"I certainly will. See you later, Dad." Mandy wound the window up. "I'll have to get one of a hamster to remind me of Frisky," she said to James and Grandad.

"Me too," James said. "That's if I can find enough space on my wall."

Mr Hope waved as they set off again for Lilac Cottage.

Back indoors, they took Frisky up to the spare room.

"Here we are." Mandy put the cage on the table. "Home safe and sound."

James peered into the cage. "You know I don't think he really cares where he is as long as he's got a nice warm nest to curl up in."

"I bet he didn't like that cold old hall, all the same." Mandy picked up the little apple branch. "Come on, let's make his playground while he's asleep."

Mandy and James carefully fixed the branch inside the cage. They hung the cotton reels from one end.

"If we tie them close together he'll be able to jump over them," Mandy said.

They did that, then they put the ladders into position. Last of all they thoroughly cleaned out the cage and filled Frisky's food bowl and water bottle.

"There," Mandy said when they had finished. "All spick and span for tomorrow."

"Tomorrow?" James said.

"He's going home," Mandy told him sadly.

"Oh," said James. "That's our holiday over, then. We haven't done much training with Blackie, have we?"

"Not really," Mandy said. "We could do some this afternoon if you like."

James bit his lip. "I think I'd rather help out at the jumble sale."

Mandy grinned. "Me too."

The following day, Mandy woke up to a strange noise. She sat up, stretched and yawned. She had oiled Frisky's wheel again so it couldn't be that.

Then she saw what it was. Frisky was racing up and down his ladders, along his apple branch and over and over his cotton reels. He was having the time of his life.

Mandy gave a little cry of delight and jumped out of bed. She sat and watched him race round and round. Eventually he stopped and took a drink from his water bottle. Then he sat washing his face. After that he just stared at Mandy for a minute or two, his little nose twitching. It was almost as if he was saying 'thank you'.

Mandy waggled her finger through the bars.

"Now you behave yourself when you get back home," she said. She opened the door and picked him up. He ran up her arm then sat on her shoulder. Mandy could see him in the mirror. He looked so bright and perky. She felt proud that she and James had looked after him so well.

She let Frisky run around a bit then put him back in his cage. "I've got to pack my bag, Frisky," she told him. "I'm going home today, too."

Mandy dressed and packed her bag. She took it downstairs. Gran and Grandad were sitting at the kitchen table.

"Home today, then?" Grandad looked up from the Sunday paper.

"Yes." Mandy sat down and helped herself to cereal. "I'm really going to miss Frisky."

"He'll miss you too, I'm sure," Gran said. She was counting the money taken at the jumble sale. "I don't suppose he's ever had so much luxury."

Mandy smiled. "He loves his adventure playground."

"Good," Gran said. "It'll be something for him to remember his holiday by."

"That's what we thought." Mandy still sounded sad.

Grandad folded up his paper. "Well, I'd better go and dig those potatoes for lunch. You staying, Mandy?"

Mandy bit her lip. She *wanted* to stay with Frisky as long as possible but she wanted to get home too. She was beginning to miss it and she was dying to see her bedroom.

Gran sat back looking pleased. "Over two hundred pounds!" she said. "That'll help with the funds for the new church roof." She looked at Grandad over the top of her glasses. "There would have been an extra fifty pence if you'd have let me sell your jumper, Tom."

Grandad gave a grunt and fumbled in his pocket. He took out a fifty-pence piece and gave it to Gran. "Oh, here you are, then." His eyes twinkled.

Gran took it and put it in the bag with

the rest of the money. "Thanks, Tom."

"When is Frisky's owner coming for him?" Mandy asked.

"This morning," Gran said. "They actually got back late last night so I should think she'll be here quite soon."

"She'll have missed Frisky, I expect," Mandy said.

"I'm sure she will. But she'll be ever so pleased he's been well looked after." Gran put her arm round Mandy. "I'm really grateful for your help, Mandy."

"It's OK, Gran."

Mandy suddenly thought of all the things she had got to do that day. She had promised to go for a walk with James and Blackie to look for conkers in Monkton Spinney. She wanted to put her books back into their bookcase and stick her posters back up on her bedroom wall. And she and James were going to read the dog training book James had got at the sale. It might have some handy hints on what to do with Blackie.

Mandy looked at her Gran. "Would

it be all right if I went home straight after breakfast?"

"Of course it would," Gran said. "Go when you like. You know you can come back any time."

"Thanks, Gran." Mandy hurriedly finished her toast then went upstairs again. Frisky was sitting on his branch. He looked a bit sleepy now.

Mandy peered through the bars. "Bye, Frisky." There was a little catch in her voice. "I hope you've enjoyed your holiday." She took him out for one last time and stroked him gently. Then, seeing how sleepy he was, she put him carefully back inside. He scrambled up to his little platform, turned and gazed at her for a minute. His whiskers twitched. Then he climbed into his nest. Soon all Mandy could see was a tight little ball of fur.

Outside, the early morning mist had cleared and the sun was shining. It was going to be a lovely autumn day. Mandy ran down the hill and along past the green. The front door of Animal Ark was open and Mrs Hope was just coming out.

"Mum!" Mandy shouted and ran up the path to meet her.

Mrs Hope gave her a hug. "Mandy! I was just going to walk up to the cottage to meet you."

"I couldn't wait to get back," said Mandy. "How's everything? How's the chinchilla?"

"He's fine. Everything's fine."

Mandy and her mum went indoors. The smell of fresh paint greeted Mandy as she ran up the stairs and burst in through

her bedroom door. She drew in her breath. It looked beautiful. Clean and fresh and bright.

Mandy sat on the bed. She thought about Frisky, all curled up snug in his little nest. She hoped he would be pleased to be going home too.

Just then her mum called from the bottom of the stairs. "Mandy, we've got a badger cub someone's brought in. Come down and see him."

Mandy leaped up. How brilliant! She had never seen a badger cub close up. She ran downstairs to join her mum.

There was no doubt about it, it had been fun staying at Hamster Hotel, but Animal Ark was the best!

Animal Ark Pets™

Mouse Magic

Mouse Magic
Special thanks to Helen Magee

Text copyright © 1996 Working Partners Ltd.
Original series created by Ben M. Baglio, London W6 0QT
Illustrations copyright © 1996 Paul Howard

First published as a single volume in Great Britain in 1997
by Hodder Children's Books

Contents

1

The Wizard of Welford

Mandy Hope ran down the track towards the low stone cottage where she lived. As she banged the garden gate shut behind her, the wooden sign above it swung in the breeze. Mandy looked up at the sign. It said 'Animal Ark'. She smiled. It was a great name for a vet's practice.

Mandy's face was flushed with excitement. She shook her short, fair hair out of her eyes and ran on down the garden path. She burst through the front door and into the house.

"Mum!" she yelled, dumping her schoolbag on the floor of the hall. "Mum, guess what!"

Mrs Hope came out of the door that led into the surgery at the end of the hall. There was another woman behind her.

"Hello, Jean," Mandy said. Jean Knox was the receptionist for Animal Ark.

"Somebody is in a rush," Jean said, smiling.

"Mandy," Mrs Hope said. "You're back early."

Mandy grinned at her mother and Jean. Emily Hope's red curly hair was tied back neatly with a green scarf and she looked cool and calm in her white lab coat. Jean's hair was ruffled and her glasses dangled on the end of their cord round her neck.

"I ran all the way home from school," Mandy said, catching her breath.

Mrs Hope smiled. "OK, what's the news?" she asked. "Come on, you can tell me while I clear up. I've just got one or two things to do in the residential unit."

"The school hall is finished," Mandy said, following her mother and Jean back through the door to the surgery.

Mrs Hope led the way to the residential unit. Mandy's parents were both vets in the little village of Welford. The residential unit was where animals were kept if they were still too sick to go home.

"The school hall?" said Mrs Hope, puzzled. "Is that what all the excitement is about?"

Mandy shook her head. "It isn't just that," she said. "Mrs Garvie says we can put on a play to celebrate – like a special opening ceremony. We started the auditions today."

Mrs Garvie was the headmistress of Welford Primary School.

"That sounds exciting," said Mrs Hope.
The telephone rang in reception.

"Don't tell all the news before I get back," called Jean as she went to answer it.

Mandy watched as her mother unhooked one of the row of cages that lined the residential unit and brought out a tiny kitten. One of his legs was in plaster.

Mandy leaned forward eagerly. "Is Snowy all right now?" she asked anxiously.

Mrs Hope nodded. "He'll be fine in a few days," she said. She tapped the kitten lightly on the nose. "And let's hope he won't go climbing trees again until he's a lot older."

"And able to get back down!" Mandy said, smiling. "Susan will be pleased."

Snowy belonged to Susan Davis. She was in the juniors at Welford Village School and Snowy was her very first pet. He had climbed up a tree in Susan's garden and got stuck. Then he'd tried to jump down and had broken his leg.

Mrs Hope put Snowy back in his cage and turned to Mandy.

"Now, tell me all about this play," she said.

Mandy clapped a hand to her mouth. "Oh, I forgot about that for a minute," she said.

Mrs Hope shook her head and laughed. "You always forget about everything else when there's an animal to be looked after."

"You can say that again," said Jean, coming into the residential unit with a pile of forms.

Mandy grinned. "But animals are so *important*," she said. "And anyway, that's just it. Mrs Garvie says we can have some animals in the play – only really well-behaved ones, of course."

Mrs Hope nodded. "I might have known it would have something to do with animals," she said. "Nothing else gets you this excited, Mandy."

"Performing animals!" Jean said, putting the pile of forms down in front of Snowy's cage. "Whatever next?"

Mandy smiled. "Oh, it's going to be wonderful," she said. "Just imagine, Mum. A school play with animals in it – isn't it terrific? Is Dad home? I want to tell him all about it, too."

Mrs Hope looked at her watch. "He should be home for tea," she said. "He's doing evening surgery later. Just let me get cleared up here and sign these forms for Jean. Then I'll make a start on tea."

"Can I help clear up?" Mandy said. Mandy loved helping out in the residential unit, even if it was just cleaning down the counters. Mr and Mrs Hope wouldn't let her actually help with the animals yet. She had to wait until she was twelve. Three whole years!

Mrs Hope handed her a bottle of disinfectant and a disposable cloth.

"Don't forget the corners," she said. "That's where the germs are."

"I won't," said Mandy, setting to work.

She scooped up a pile of forms from in front of Snowy's cage. The little kitten had one paw through the bars and was steadily edging the papers off the counter.

"Something tells me that kitten is going to be quite a handful when he grows up," said Mrs Hope, laughing. "You'd better give those to me, Mandy."

By the time Mandy had cleaned down

all the counters – and talked to all the animals – Mrs Hope had finished the medications and signed all the forms.

"Oh," said Mandy, "I forgot. James is coming for tea. Is that all right? He's got some extra special news about the play."

Mrs Hope smiled. "James is always welcome," she said. "You go and get changed."

"I'll just file these and be off," said Jean, collecting the forms. "Put my name down for a ticket for the play, Mandy."

"I will," Mandy promised. "I'll get you a seat in the very front row!"

Mandy changed into jeans and a T-shirt in double quick time. She heard her father's deep voice as she came downstairs into the kitchen.

"Look who I found outside," said Mr Hope, his dark eyes twinkling.

"James!" said Mandy, looking at the boy standing beside her dad. He had floppy

brown hair and glasses that were halfway down his nose. A young black Labrador fidgeted beside him.

James Hunter was a year younger than Mandy. He was her best friend. The Labrador gave a short bark and launched himself at Mandy on his long, gangly legs. Mandy giggled and rubbed his ears.

"Oh, Blackie," she said. "Have you come for tea as well?"

James blushed. "I tried to make him stay at home," he said.

"That's all right," Mr Hope said, laughing. "After all, this *is* Animal Ark."

"As if we wouldn't want to see Blackie," Mandy said. "Come on, James, let's lay the table. Then we can tell all our news."

"Salad tonight," Mrs Hope said, going to the fridge.

Mandy and James laid the big pine table in the middle of the kitchen while Mrs Hope took bowls of salad, hard boiled eggs and quiche from the fridge.

"That looks good," said Mr Hope as they all sat down. "Now, what's this news?"

James and Mandy began to speak at once and Mr Hope held up his hand. "One at a time," he said.

Mandy started to tell her dad all about the school hall and the play.

"The play is going to be called *The Wizard of Welford*," she said.

"It's all about a wizard who comes to Welford and shows people how clever animals are," said James.

"And there's a baddie," said Mandy. "Horrible Horace. Andrew Pearson is going to play him because he's the tallest boy in school."

"Horace is really bad to animals and the wizard has to find a way to show him how cruel he is," said James.

"Only we haven't got that bit quite right yet," Mandy said.

"We've been working on the story all day at school," James said.

"Gary Roberts wants to frighten Horrible Horace with Gertie," Mandy said.

Mr Hope laughed. "Gertie is only a garter snake," he said. "It doesn't sound as though she'll be enough to frighten Horrible Horace."

James nodded. "That's what the rest of us said," he replied. "So Gary is going to be a snake charmer in the play instead."

"Maybe he could put a spell on Horrible Horace," Mrs Hope suggested.

Mandy shook her head. "Snake charmers only put spells on snakes," she said. "What we need is a special spell for the wizard to put on Horrible Horace."

"You'll think of something," Mr Hope said.

Mandy nodded. "I hope so," she said. "We also need a better ending for the play."

"And when we think of it, we'll keep it as a surprise," said James. "We won't tell anyone before the play."

Mandy grinned. "If we think of

something," she said. "But the really *terrific* news is about the wizard." She turned to James. "Tell them!"

James blushed. "You tell them," he mumbled, pushing his glasses up his nose.

Mandy turned to her parents. "James is going to be the wizard!" she said.

"Congratulations, James," said Mrs Hope warmly.

James blushed even more. "I've got to learn to do magic tricks," he said. "I got a book out of the school library but it looks difficult. I'll need to practise really hard. Did Mandy tell you she's got a part too?"

"Oops!" said Mandy to her parents. "I was so busy telling you about the animals, I forgot. I'm the wizard's apprentice."

"Well done, Mandy," Mrs Hope said. "I'm sure you and James will make a great team."

"The Wizard of Welford," Mr Hope said. "Maybe you can put a spell on Blackie."

Mandy and James looked round at the

black Labrador. Blackie was lying in the corner of the kitchen quietly chewing one of Mr Hope's slippers.

"Blackie!" James yelled, making a dive for him.

"Uh-oh," said Mandy. "If Blackie is quiet it always means he's up to something."

Blackie looked up and put his head on one side. The slipper dangled from his mouth. His big dark eyes looked innocent.

Mrs Hope laughed. "I think it would take more than a wizard to train Blackie," she said.

James got the slipper away from Blackie and held it up. "It's a bit of a mess, Mr Hope," he said.

"It's high time Mandy's dad had a new pair of slippers anyway," Mrs Hope said. "I've been trying to get rid of those for ages. You've done me a big favour, James. In fact, it's magic!"

"You see," said Mandy. "It's working already. James really *is* a wizard!"

2

Mr Spellini

"You'll need a wizard's costume," Mandy said to James as they helped clear away the tea things.

"You mean like a pointy hat and a cloak?" said James.

Mandy nodded. "A cloak with things like stars and moons on it," she said.

"Why don't you ask Gran to help?" Mrs Hope said. "You know how good she is at things like that."

"Brilliant," Mandy said. "I was going to talk to her about my costume anyway. Let's go now, James."

Mr Hope stacked a pile of plates on the draining-board. "See if you can come up with a spell that makes dishes wash themselves, James," he said.

Mandy grinned. "Is that a hint for us to help with the washing-up?" she asked.

Mrs Hope turned the tap on. "No, it isn't," she said. "Off you go!"

"Come on, Blackie. Walkies!" Mandy said.

Blackie leaped up and lolloped to the door.

"Abracadabra!" Mr Hope said to the pile of plates, waving the washing-up brush.

Mandy laughed and shot out of the door with James and Blackie.

"See you later," she called back.

Mandy's gran and grandad lived at Lilac Cottage, not far from Animal Ark. Mandy and James passed Hobart's Corner on the way.

Mandy looked through the gates at the house as they passed. The windows and the fresh white paint shone in the evening sunlight. The garden was full of flowers and the grass had been newly-mown.

"Hobart's Corner is looking really great now," she said.

James nodded. "I always thought it looked spooky," he admitted. "But only because it was empty for so long."

Jack Gardiner and his parents had moved into the house at Hobart's Corner two months ago. They were turning it into a guest house. Jack was seven and had a pet rabbit called Hoppy.

"I wonder how Hoppy is," Mandy said.

"We could go and visit him," said James.

Mandy shook her head. "Maybe later. Let's see about your costume first."

They found Gran and Grandad in the back garden of Lilac Cottage. Grandad was working on his vegetable patch and Gran was picking strawberries. Mandy's Grandad was a champion vegetable grower.

"Hi, Gran! Hi, Grandad!" Mandy called as she and James came through the gate.

Grandad looked up as Blackie bounded over to him.

"Hello, young fellow," Grandad said, giving Blackie a pat.

"You two are just in time," Gran said to Mandy and James. "Come and help me pick some strawberries."

Mandy and James grinned. Their favourite task!

"Three for the basket and one for the picker," Mandy said.

Gran smiled. "That's the best way to pick them."

Mandy and James each took a basket from the garage and started picking.

"Gran," said Mandy, "James and I wanted to ask you a favour."

"Oho!" said Grandad. "You've found a stray puppy and you want us to take it in."

Mandy looked at Blackie. The Labrador was lying contentedly on the ground while Grandad tickled his tummy.

"No," she said. "We want Gran to make a costume for James, please. And one for me, if she's got time."

Mandy explained all about the play while she, James and Gran worked their way down the row of strawberries. The fruit smelled sweet. Mandy finished explaining and popped a plump, juicy fruit into her mouth.

"Mmm," she said. "These are scrummy!"

"Let's go inside and you can have a bowl of them with some cream," Gran said. "Your costume should be easy enough, Mandy. A tunic would do. But we should try out some designs for James's costume."

"So, you'll do it?" said James.

Gran smiled. "I'd love to make a wizard's costume," she said.

"And I'd love some strawberries and cream," Grandad said, leaning on his hoe. "Gardening is hard work."

Mandy laughed as they all trooped inside.

Gran got some paper and pencils and they all sat round the kitchen table with their bowls of fruit, discussing James's costume.

"That was great," said Mandy, scraping up the last of the cream with her spoon.

"And just look at the design for my costume," James said. Mandy looked at the sheet of paper in front of Gran. She had drawn a long flowing cloak covered with stars and moons.

"I'll use silver paper for the decorations," Gran said, "and plenty of sequins."

"I'll make you a long black moustache, James," said Grandad. "It'll make you look mysterious."

"And we'll need a hat," said Mandy. "James and I can make one from black card and stick more sequins on it."

"Now, about your costume, Mandy," Gran said. "What exactly do you have to do in the play? Do you need to be able to run around?"

Mandy grinned. "Oh, yes! I'm the wizard's apprentice," she said. "I've got to set the bravest dog in the village on Horrible Horace to save my master."

"Guess who the dog is?" said James.

"Don't tell us – Blackie," said Grandad.

James nodded. "Mrs Garvie asked for him specially."

Blackie looked up and gave a short bark.

"The only trouble will be training him to *stop* chasing Andrew Pearson," Mandy said, giving Blackie's ears a rub.

"Blackie has to get the wizard's wand back when Horrible Horace steals it," said James. "It's a very important part in the play. The wizard is powerless without his wand."

"We're going to try to include all the pets we can," said Mandy. "It's going to be wonderful."

"Jill Redfern is going to bring Toto, her tortoise," said James.

"And then there's Duchess, Richard Tanner's Persian cat," said Mandy.

"And Laura Baker's rabbits," said James. "And Amy Fenton is going to do some gymnastics. She's really excited."

"Amy was upset that Minnie couldn't have a part," Mandy explained. "But Mrs Garvie didn't see how we could fit a mouse into the story."

"That's why Amy is doing some gymnastics instead," James said.

"Is Jack Gardiner's rabbit, Hoppy, going to be in the play?" Gran asked.

James nodded. "Mmm. We're going to go and see Jack on the way home," he said.

"And Hoppy," Mandy added.

"Don't get in the way," Gran said. "Mrs Gardiner is expecting her very first paying guest today and she's really excited. She wants everything to be just right. They've worked so hard getting Hobart's Corner fixed up."

"We won't get in the way," said Mandy, getting up from the table. "Thanks for the strawberries, Gran."

"And for agreeing to make the costume and the moustache," said James.

"Come on, Blackie," Mandy said. "Let's go and see if Mrs Gardiner's paying guest has brought a pet."

Mandy and James found Jack playing with Hoppy in the garden at Hobart's Corner. The black and white rabbit looked up at them with his bright black eyes. He wasn't at all afraid of Mandy and James. He knew them so well.

"Hi, Hoppy!" Mandy said, tickling the

little animal behind the ears.

Hoppy sat up on his hind legs and began to wash his whiskers. Jack held out a lettuce leaf and Hoppy sniffed at it, then nibbled delicately.

"He's getting so big," Mandy said.

Jack stretched out a hand and stroked his rabbit. "Laura says he's even bigger than Patch," he said.

Laura Baker had three rabbits – Nibbles, Fluffy and Patch. Patch was from the same

litter as Hoppy. Jack hadn't wanted a pet when he first came to Welford but as soon as he saw Fluffy's babies being born he fell in love with them. So Laura had asked him if he wanted one and Jack had chosen Hoppy.

"Gran says you're getting your first paying guest," said Mandy. "Do you know who it is?"

Jack shook his head. "He should be arriving any time. I'm watching for him. Mum says his name is Mr Spellini. But she doesn't know anything else about him."

"What an odd name," said James.

Mandy heard a car draw up at the gate and turned quickly.

"It's a taxi," said James. "It must be him."

Mandy, James and Jack watched as the taxi turned into the drive and stopped at the front door.

"Can you see him?" asked Jack.

"Wait a minute. He's getting out," Mandy said.

They watched as a tall, thin man stepped out of the taxi. He stood for a moment looking round the garden. Mandy drew in her breath. He looked extraordinary. He was wearing a long black cape and he had a top hat on. They could see very dark eyes and a pointed black beard. He was carrying what looked like two big covered boxes with handles on top. He put them down very carefully on the front steps of the house.

"Cripes!" James gulped. "Look at those clothes."

"They are a bit odd!" said Mandy. "I wonder what's in the boxes."

Jack's eyes were large, round saucers.

Mr Spellini walked round to the back of the taxi as the driver opened the boot. He reached in and lifted out a big black trunk. He put the trunk on the ground and the taxi drove off. Then he looked round the garden – and saw them.

Mandy felt her eyes popping as he swept

off his top hat and bowed to them. His cape swirled about him. Then he turned and disappeared into the house.

"Wow!" said James. "Who do you think he is?"

Mandy was looking at the trunk. It was very big and very black and it had a huge lock on it.

"And what do you think is in the trunk?" she asked.

"I don't know," James said. "But I've never seen anybody like Mr Spellini before."

3

Magic at the post-office

For the next few days, Mandy and James were really busy rehearsing the play. On Friday afternoon they were on stage in the middle of more rehearsals. All the children were there. James had brought Blackie specially so that they could rehearse his part. Mrs Todd and Mrs Black, James and

Mandy's teachers, were in charge.

James was still thinking about the mysterious Mr Spellini and his locked trunk. Jack hadn't found out what was in it and James's imagination was running away with him.

"Maybe Mr Spellini's got a body stashed away in the trunk," he said, rolling his eyes dramatically so that his glasses slid right down his nose.

"Or stacks of money from a bank robbery," said Mandy.

"Shh! Here comes Mrs Garvie," warned Jill Redfern behind them.

"You've all done very well so far," said Mrs Garvie as she came up on to the stage. "But I want you to practise hard all next week as well. The big day is a week from Saturday and I want everything perfect for then."

"I'll never get Gertie ready by then," said Gary Roberts.

Mrs Garvie gave him a weary look. "It

isn't Gertie you need to worry about, Gary," she said. "What *you* need to do is practise your tune on the recorder."

Everybody laughed. Gary wasn't very good at playing the recorder.

"I'm getting quite good at being Horrible Horace," Andrew Pearson said. He growled at little Laura Baker. "Get out of my way or your rabbits will end up in a rabbit pie," he snarled.

"Huh!" said Laura. "You'll have to do better than that. Even Patch wouldn't be frightened of *that* and Fluffy would probably bite you."

"How are your magic tricks coming on, James?" Mrs Garvie asked.

James bit his lip. "Not very well, Mrs Garvie," he said. "It's really hard to learn tricks from a book."

"I'm sure you'll manage with practice," said Mrs Garvie. "Mandy can help you."

"We're going to get some playing-cards from the post-office," Mandy said. "Card tricks might not be so difficult."

Mrs Garvie looked at Blackie sitting at James's feet. "And how's Blackie getting on with his part?"

Blackie had to chase Horrible Horace round the stage. Then Horrible Horace had to throw the wizard's wand away and Blackie had to retrieve it and bring it to Mandy.

"He's very good at the chasing bit," Mandy said.

"Too right," Andrew said. "He wouldn't stop chasing me last time we practised. And when he retrieved the wand, he brought it back to me instead of taking it to Mandy."

"That's because he's trained to give the stick back to whoever throws it," said James.

"Oh, I've got an idea that should solve that," said Mandy. She held up a packet of dog biscuits.

"What are those for?" said Andrew.

"I'm going to try rattling the dog biscuits

when he retrieves the wand," she said. "I bet Blackie would rather have a biscuit than come back to you with a stick, Andrew."

"That's a good idea," said Mrs Garvie.

Andrew didn't look convinced.

"At least Blackie's got a part," Amy Fenton said. "Poor Minnie hasn't got a part at all."

Mrs Garvie shook her head. "It's a little difficult to think of a part for a white mouse," she said. "And I wouldn't want Duchess to scare her."

Duchess, Richard Tanner's Persian cat, was huge. She would scare the life out of Minnie.

"At least I can do my gymnastics," Amy said as Mrs Garvie went to speak to another group of pupils. "But I'm still sorry for poor Minnie."

Mandy smiled at her. "Why don't you ask Mrs Garvie if you can bring Minnie to the pets rehearsal next week? As long as you keep her in her cage Duchess won't harm her."

Amy cheered up. "That's a good idea," she said. "I'll do that. She'd like to see the play."

"Now back to work," Mrs Todd said. "We've still got a lot to do. Let's try Blackie's part – with the dog biscuits this time."

Andrew took his place centre stage as the villagers cowered in fear before him. James lay down at Mandy's feet.

Mandy put her hand lightly on Blackie's collar, keeping him close to her. Then she turned to Andrew.

"Look what you have done to my master!" she cried. "You have stolen his wand. You have stolen his power!"

Andrew raised the wizard's magic wand.

"And now I'm going to turn all your pets to stone," he snarled.

Mandy dropped to one knee and gave Blackie a little push. "Go, Blackie," she said urgently. "Get Andrew!"

Blackie trotted forward and Andrew threw his hands in the air and began to run away from the dog. Once, twice, three times round the stage. Then Andrew flung the wand high in the air. Blackie looked up. He watched the stick turn and twist as it fell towards him. He made a leap and caught it.

Quickly Mandy pulled out the packet of dog biscuits and rattled them. Blackie's

ears pricked as he heard the familiar sound. He turned and looked at Mandy.

"Here, boy," she whispered.

Blackie ran towards her and Mandy grabbed the wand and gave Blackie his reward. Blackie crunched the biscuit as the rest of the cast started to clap.

"It worked," said Mrs Garvie. "Well done, Mandy!"

Mandy flushed with pleasure. "Well done, Blackie," she said to the Labrador.

By the time school was over, Mandy and James were very proud of Blackie. James clipped on the Labrador's lead as they walked through the school gates.

"You were great, boy," he said, giving Blackie a pat.

Mandy laughed. "I think the dog biscuits helped," she said.

"One thing's for sure," James said. "Blackie is going to really like rehearsing now that he knows he gets biscuits as a reward."

"I'll just have to make sure he doesn't get too many," Mandy said, "or he'll get fat."

"Let's see if Mrs McFarlane has those playing-cards I need for my magic tricks," James said as they reached the post-office.

"Mrs McFarlane has everything," Mandy said as they pushed open the door and went in.

The post-office was their favourite shop in the village. It sold all kinds of things – comics and sweets, games and books. Mandy was so busy looking at the animal magazines by the door that she didn't notice when James suddenly stopped dead.

"Ouch!" she said, bumping into him. "What's the matter?"

"Look!" James said. "It's him."

Mandy looked across at the post-office counter. Mr Spellini, the mysterious guest at Hobart's Corner, was buying stamps, his black cape thrown over one shoulder. Mrs

McFarlane looked over to Mandy and James and smiled.

"I won't be a moment," she said.

"That's all right, Mrs McFarlane," Mandy said. "We'll just have a look around. James is looking for playing-cards."

"I have to learn some magic tricks," James explained with a grin.

"You'll find them on the far wall, bottom shelf," Mrs McFarlane said and turned back to the counter.

As James walked over to search for them, Mandy saw Mr Spellini turning to look at them. He seemed very interested in what they were doing. Then her attention was caught by a shelf of toys in the corner of the shop and she forgot all about him.

"Hey, James," she called, picking up a box from the shelf. "Look what I've found."

James came over, a pack of playing-cards in his hand.

"Magic tricks!" he said, reading the label

on the box. "These look terrific."

The shop doorbell rang as a large woman with an extraordinary hat perched right on top of her head came bustling into the shop. She carried an overweight Pekinese under one arm.

It was Mrs Ponsonby, the bossiest woman in Welford. Blackie lolloped over and tried to make friends with the Pekinese, but it only yapped at him.

"Good afternoon, Mandy," Mrs Ponsonby said. Then, before Mandy could reply, she caught sight of James with the pack of cards in his hand.

"Playing-cards!" she said. "James Hunter, I hope you are not taking to card games!"

James tried to say something but Mrs Ponsonby took no notice.

"And what else do you have there?" she asked, peering at the box in his other hand. "Magic tricks! What a waste of money! You should be buying something educational instead of spending money on tricks."

Mandy saw a movement out of the corner of her eye. She looked round. Mr Spellini turned from the post-office counter, his black cape swirling around him. For a moment he looked straight at Mandy. His eyes sparkled and he gave her a wink. Then he swept up to Mrs Ponsonby and bowed.

"You do not like magic tricks, Madam?" he said.

Mrs Ponsonby looked startled. "I don't like surprises," she said. "Not that any trick could surprise me. I'm not easily taken in, you know."

Mr Spellini spread his hands wide. "Are you never surprised?" he said. "Not even when you find something strange behind your ear?"

"Behind my ear?" Mrs Ponsonby screeched. "What on earth are you talking about?"

Mr Spellini smiled widely and stretched out his hand. Before Mrs Ponsonby could say another word, Mr Spellini put his hand

behind her ear and drew out an egg.

"Wow!" said James, his mouth dropping open. "Did you see that?"

"How did he do it?" said Mandy.

"Magic!" James breathed.

Mrs Ponsonby's eyes popped. "Where did you get that?" she said, staring at the egg in Mr Spellini's hand.

Mr Spellini smiled. "From behind your ear," he said. He put his head on one side. "A surprising place to keep an egg."

And, with another bow, he swept out of the shop, his cape billowing behind him.

"Well!" said Mrs Ponsonby at last. "Did you ever see anything as rude as that in your life? An egg behind my ear! What a cheek."

Mandy and James stood there, their mouths clamped shut, trying not to laugh.

Mrs McFarlane's eyes were as round as saucers.

"Well," she said. "I must say that Mr Spellini is a strange one. You don't see many top hats and capes in Welford – and as for taking eggs out of people's ears, I've never seen the like of it!"

"Hmmph," said Mrs Ponsonby. "If you ask me, there's something funny about that man. Anybody that goes around in a big black cape just has to be suspicious. I think he's a spy."

"A spy?" said Mrs McFarlane. "Why on earth would a spy come to Welford?"

"On a secret mission," Mrs Ponsonby said.

Mandy and James looked at each other.

"A secret mission?" Mandy whispered. "Mrs Ponsonby must read some pretty weird books."

"If she thinks spies dress like that she must do," James replied. "Mr Spellini isn't a spy. He's a magician!"

4

The mystery trunk

Mandy and James paid for their things while Mrs Ponsonby went on and on about spies. Poor Mrs McFarlane couldn't get a word in. Mrs Ponsonby was still talking as they made their escape.

"Did you see Mrs Ponsonby's face?" James said, whooping with laughter as they left the post-office behind them.

"I thought she was going to explode," said Mandy. She could hardly walk for laughing. "An egg! Oh, I wish I'd had a camera."

"And she thinks he's a spy," said James. "Anybody can see he's a magician."

Mandy looked thoughtful. "I wonder if Jack knows that," she said. "Let's go along to Hobart's Corner and see what we can find out."

"About Mr Spellini?" James asked.

Mandy nodded. "*We'll* be the spies," she said, grinning.

They didn't get as far as the garden gates at Hobart's Corner. Halfway along the high garden wall Mandy stopped and looked around.

"Did you hear something?" she said.

James shook his head. Then the sound came again.

"Psst!" said a voice above their heads.

Mandy and James looked up. Jack was

sprawled along the top of the garden wall.

"What are you doing up there?" said James.

Jack's face was lit up with excitement. "I've found out what's in Mr Spellini's trunk," he exclaimed. "It's amazing! Come and see."

James made for the gate but Jack called him back.

"Up here, on the wall," the little boy said. "I've got a great view."

Mandy and James scrambled up the wall and perched beside Jack.

"What about Blackie?" asked Mandy, looking down at the Labrador.

Blackie looked up at her and scampered off in the direction of the gate.

"Blackie!" Mandy called softly but he paid no attention to her.

"Wow!" said James. "Look at that, Mandy."

Mandy looked where James was pointing. There was an apple tree right next to the wall and she had to twist round to see through the leaves. Then she saw why Jack was so excited.

Mr Spellini was standing in the middle of the garden. There were two empty cages at his feet. One of them looked like a bird cage. The big black trunk stood wide open on the grass in front of him.

"He must have animals and birds," Mandy said softly. "Those boxes were really pet cages."

"He's got a rabbit," Jack said. "He bought a hutch from the pet shop in Walton for it and Dad's put it beside Hoppy's hutch. He's got doves, too, but he keeps them in that big bird cage in his room."

As they watched, Mr Spellini took a little table out of the trunk and set it on the grass. He took out a vase, then waved his hands in the air. Suddenly he was holding a bunch of flowers. He popped the flowers into the vase and put the vase on the table.

Mandy gasped with delight. "Where did they come from?" she said.

"I wish I could learn to do that for the play," James said.

"Isn't he great?" said Jack, his eyes shining.

Mr Spellini started to pull a long string of coloured flags out of his mouth and draped them across the table.

"Did you see what he did with those flags?" said James. "It must take years to learn how to do that."

Then Mr Spellini took off his top hat – and pulled out a rabbit! He set the rabbit on the table in front of him beside the flowers. The little animal settled down comfortably and began to clean its whiskers.

"Look! That's his rabbit," said Jack, delighted.

"But where are the doves?" Mandy said.

At that moment Blackie came dashing through the garden gate and raced across the grass. Mr Spellini picked up the rabbit – and it disappeared. He threw his hands in the air and four white doves fluttered into the sky. Blackie stopped and looked up. Then he started chasing the doves across the garden.

Mr Spellini turned round and bowed to them.

"He's seen us," said Jack.

Mr Spellini waved his hands twice in the air and the doves came fluttering back and settled on his arms. One of them picked its way delicately up his sleeve and sat on the magician's shoulder.

"You can come down now," Mr Spellini called to them. "I hope you enjoyed the little show."

Mandy, James and Jack scrambled down from the wall.

"We weren't really spying on you," said James, blushing.

Mr Spellini laughed. "It's all right," he said, walking towards them. "I knew Jack was there and I thought I would give him a treat."

"That was brilliant, Mr Spellini," Jack said.

"Uh-oh!" said James as Blackie lolloped across the grass towards them.

Mr Spellini gathered the doves together and put them into the bird cage, closing the door very gently. Then he hung the cage on a branch of the apple tree, well out of Blackie's reach.

"Oh, they're beautiful," Mandy breathed, looking at the doves. The birds ruffled their soft white feathers and settled down.

"How do you train them?" James asked.

Mr Spellini waved his hand over the birds. A river of corn fell from his fingers and dropped into the cage.

"With kindness and rewards," he said. "It's the only way to train animals."

"I wish you could teach me a thing or two about training animals," James said, collaring Blackie.

Mr Spellini stroked his beard. "And perhaps magic tricks as well?"

James looked up at the magician, his mouth open.

Mr Spellini turned to Mandy. "When I saw you in the post-office, you said James had to learn some magic tricks," he said.

Mandy nodded. "We're putting on a school play," she said. "James is going to be the Wizard of Welford. He has to do tricks. We're going to have some animals in the play as well."

Mr Spellini smiled. "And when is this play?" he said.

James bit his lip. "Next Saturday," he said. "We don't have much time."

Mr Spellini shook his head. "What you need is a little bit of magic," he said.

Mandy smiled. "Would you help us, Mr Spellini?" she asked.

Mr Spellini bowed. "I'd be delighted," he said. "It will be useful for me, too. A magician has to practise, you know. Even when he is on holiday."

"That would be brilliant," James said.

Mr Spellini looked at Jack, who had a puzzled frown on his face. "What do you think, Jack?" he said.

"I was wondering about the rabbit," he said. "The one that disappeared."

Mr Spellini laughed and reached under his cape. He brought out the rabbit and handed it to Jack.

"You see," he said. "He's perfectly safe and well."

Jack cuddled the rabbit and looked up at Mr Spellini. "There are rabbits in the play," he said. "I'm sure you'll like them."

"I'm sure I will too," said Mr Spellini. "But we must get to work if James is to turn into a wizard by next Saturday. That will take quite a lot of magic."

Mandy looked at Mr Spellini. "Oh, you can do it," she said. "I just know you can."

5

Disaster

The first thing Mr Spellini wanted to see was James's costume. He would not explain to Mandy why it was so important but just looked mysterious. After that, of course, he wanted to meet Mrs Garvie and get her permission to help.

Mandy and James arranged to take Mr

Spellini round to Lilac Cottage after tea so that he could see Gran's design for James's costume. Back at Animal Ark Mandy was so excited she could hardly eat her meal, for talking about Mr Spellini.

Mrs Hope phoned Jack's mother and came back all smiles.

"Mr Spellini has been showing the Gardiners some of his press cuttings," she said. "He's quite famous, you know."

"I think he's wonderful," said Mandy.

"He was also asking about a vet," said Mrs Hope. "One of his doves isn't eating so I've promised to go round and have a look at it. I'll drive you all round to Gran and Grandad's afterwards."

"Maybe Mr Spellini will show you some tricks," Mandy said. Then she frowned. "I hope the dove isn't sick."

When Mandy and Mrs Hope arrived at Hobart's Corner, Mr Spellini was too concerned about his dove to do tricks for them. Mandy could see by his worried face that he really loved his animals.

Mrs Hope took the bird expertly in her hands. She ran her fingers carefully over its breast and up towards its throat. Then she pressed gently on each side of the dove's neck and watched as the bird tried to swallow.

"What's her name, Mr Spellini?" Mandy asked.

The magician was watching Mrs Hope intently. "Bianca," he said without taking his eyes off her.

Mrs Hope finished examining Bianca and frowned slightly.

"There seems to be something in her throat," she said. "I'll have to take her into Animal Ark and have a closer look."

Mr Spellini nodded and fetched a travelling cage for the dove.

"Bianca is a very clever bird," he said, closing the latch of the cage carefully. "I'd be lost without her."

Mrs Hope smiled. "I imagine she's a very

valuable bird as well," she said.

Mr Spellini nodded. "She is very special."

Mrs Hope took the cage gently from him. "I'm sure she'll be fine, Mr Spellini," she said. "I'll be able to let you know how she is once I've examined her more thoroughly."

Mr Spellini nodded again but Mandy could see he was still worried as they all got into the car.

Mrs Hope called for James and then drove them all to Lilac Cottage.

As they walked down the path towards the cottage, Gran came out of the front door.

"Gran," said Mandy, "this is Mr Spellini. He's a magician and he's going to help James with some magic tricks."

Gran looked at Mr Spellini and her face lit up.

"The Spectacular Spellini!" she said. "I saw you last year in York. You were very good."

Mr Spellini bowed, drew a coloured scarf magically from between his fingers and presented it to Gran.

"Well," said Gran. "It certainly must be very useful being a magician. I'm always losing scarves. It would be nice to conjure one up just like that when I needed it."

Mandy smiled but she was still thinking about Bianca.

"Are you sure she'll be all right?" she whispered to her mother.

Mrs Hope smiled reassuringly. "Don't worry. It's probably just something stuck in her throat."

They followed Gran indoors and soon Mr Spellini was examining James's costume inside and out. "As I thought," he said. "Not enough pockets." He looked at James "Magicians need lots of pockets."

Gran, James and Mr Spellini went into a huddle over the costume while Grandad brought a selection of fresh vegetables in from the garden for Mrs Hope.

"You don't get those by waving a magic wand!" Mrs Hope said.

Grandad scratched his head. "It's a different kind of magic, getting things to grow," he said.

At last Mr Spellini was satisfied with the new design for the costume and Mrs Hope drove him back to Hobart's Corner.

"Come round about eight o'clock this evening," she said. "You'll be able to see Bianca then."

Mr Spellini said he would, but, as they drove off, Mandy could see he was still very concerned.

Back at Animal Ark, Mandy hung around outside the room used as an operating theatre while Mrs Hope examined Bianca. Simon, the veterinary nurse for the practice, was on hand to help.

It seemed like hours before Simon poked his head outside. "All over now," he said, smiling at Mandy.

She hurried inside.

"You can stop worrying now," said her mother. "Bianca had a rather large seed stuck deep down in her throat. I removed it while she was asleep. She'll feel a bit sore for a little while but she'll be as right as rain in a day or two."

Mandy walked over to the operating table and looked down at the beautiful white dove just beginning to stir. Her eyelids fluttered slightly.

"We'll keep her in overnight," Mrs

Hope said, "and she'll be able to go home tomorrow."

"And will she really be all right?" said Mandy.

"She'll be the star of Mr Spellini's next show, you wait and see," Mrs Hope said.

Mandy smiled. She would have good news for Mr Spellini.

When Mr Spellini arrived, he was full of thanks and very relieved to see Bianca looking well again.

"Mum says she'll be the star of your show again in no time," Mandy said to him.

Mr Spellini smiled. "I hope so," he said. "She loves performing."

"Isn't she frightened by all the crowds?" Mandy said.

"Not at all," said Mr Spellini. "She's used to it now."

Mandy frowned. "I'm a bit worried in case some of the animals in the play will be frightened," she said.

Mr Spellini looked serious. "You must be sure that all the pets are able to stay close to their owners," he said. "That will give them confidence. It's also a good idea to have a quiet place backstage for them when they're not on stage." He hesitated. "I could speak to Mrs Garvie about the arrangements for the animals."

Mandy smiled. "Would you?" she said. "That would be great. It would be terrible if any of the pets got frightened. It's the pets' rehearsal on Monday morning. All the animals will be there."

"Then I'll come along on Monday as well," said Mr Spellini.

Mandy smiled. "Thanks, Mr Spellini," she said. "That would be terrific."

On Monday morning Mrs Garvie took Mr Spellini into her office for a long chat about the arrangements for the pets – and, of course, James's tricks. Then she gathered the cast of the play together for the pets' rehearsal.

"We are very lucky to have a real magician to help us," she said to them. "Mr Spellini is going to come to all our rehearsals — and he's going to teach James some magic tricks."

Amy Fenton jumped up and down. "Oh good," she said to James. "And then you can show us how they're done, James."

James shook his head, looking serious. "No, I can't," he said. "Mr Spellini says I have to promise to keep the tricks secret."

Amy looked disappointed. But she soon brightened up. She had Minnie with her and she remembered she was going to do her whole gymnastic routine for the first time today. She was supposed to be the wizard's pet monkey and they all had to imagine her in a monkey costume.

Everybody cheered like mad when Amy did her gymnastics. She really was good. She did somersaults and backflips. She even did the splits. She looked really proud when she finished.

Then it was Gary's turn with Gertie. But poor Gary just wasn't any good at the recorder.

"That doesn't matter," said Mr Spellini. "Who *is* good at the recorder?"

Pam Stanton put her hand in the air. "I am," she said. "But I've got a part in the play already with Ginny, my guinea-pig. And anyway, Gary really likes being the snake charmer."

"But Gary can still be the snake charmer," Mr Spellini said to Pam. "You can play the recorder offstage while Gary mimes."

Gary looked puzzled. "But won't Gertie go looking for the music?"

Mr Spellini shook his head. "You can't actually charm snakes, you know," he said gently. "But you could *pretend* you were charming Gertie. You could hold the recorder with one hand, lift Gertie up with the other and sway about as if she was dancing."

Gary's face lit up. "Oh, that's no problem. I'll be OK at swaying. It's just the playing I'm rubbish at."

Everybody laughed. Except Amy. She had just looked down at Minnie's cage which was sitting on a low table on the stage. It was empty.

"Minnie!" she said. "Oh, where's Minnie? She's escaped!"

"Oh, no!" said Richard Tanner. "I haven't put Duchess back in her basket yet. Where is she?"

Mandy looked round the stage. "There, look!" she said as the Persian cat streaked across the floor. Mandy had never seen Duchess move so fast.

Something small and white scampered across the stage towards the curtain at the side.

"There's Minnie!" Amy wailed and the little girl made a dash for the corner of the stage.

Minnie ran up the curtain and on to the top of a piece of scenery. Duchess stood at the bottom, ready to spring. But before the cat could do anything, Amy scrambled up the wall, edged out along the scenery and stretched out her hand towards Minnie.

Richard pounced on Duchess, scooped her into his arms and put her back in her basket.

"Watch out, Amy!" Mrs Garvie called.

But it was too late. The scenery toppled forward just as Amy grasped Minnie. Amy, Minnie and the scenery came down with a crash.

Mandy was the first to reach them.

"Oh, is Minnie all right?" Amy said.

Mandy scooped up the little mouse before she could run off again and held her securely.

"I've got her. She's fine," she said. "What about you?"

Amy started to get to her feet. "I'm fine – ouch!" she said. "My ankle hurts!"

Mrs Garvie arrived.

"Lie still, Amy," she said. "Are you all right?"

"Oh, my ankle," Amy wailed.

Mrs Garvie felt Amy's ankle gently. Then she sat back with a sigh of relief.

"I don't think it's broken," she said. "But it's probably sprained. We'll have to get the nurse to take a look at you."

She looked at Amy and shook her head. "I'm afraid there won't be any gymnastics for you for a while, Amy," she said.

Amy looked up. Two big tears came into her eyes and spilled over.

"Oh, no!" she said. "And Minnie doesn't have a part either."

Mandy looked down at the mouse, sitting quietly in her hands. Minnie seemed none the worse for her adventure. She put the little animal back in her cage.

"At least Minnie isn't hurt," Mandy said, trying to cheer Amy up.

Amy looked up at her and nodded. She

was very white. Her ankle must be really painful.

"Oh, I know," she said. "I don't really mind anything so long as Minnie is all right. I'm just a bit disappointed, that's all. I was really looking forward to being in the play."

Mandy smiled and handed the cage to her. Amy was being very brave about all this. Mandy just wished she could wave James's magic wand and make her ankle better.

6

Spellini to the rescue

The next week was really busy. There were rehearsals every day at school and every evening after tea James went round to Hobart's Corner to work with Mr Spellini. And each day, James was looking a bit more confident about his magic tricks.

So far he'd learned how to make a ping

pong ball disappear from right under Mandy's nose and how to turn a box of torn-up newspaper into a whole page again just by tapping on the box with Mr Spellini's wand. He was amazing!

Mandy had been round to Hobart's Corner with James once or twice but she hadn't been allowed to see how the tricks were done. Mr Spellini was very serious about keeping the tricks a secret.

On Thursday, the two friends visited Amy after school. They found her sitting in a garden chair looking miserable, with her foot propped up in front of her. Minnie's cage was on the grass beside her.

"Doctor Prescott says I can go back to school tomorrow," she said. "But I won't be able to do any gymnastics for ages."

Mandy and James sat down on the grass.

"Susan Davis is going to be the monkey now," Mandy said.

Amy nodded. "Susan is in my gymnastics class," she said. "She'll be really good."

"At least you'll be able to come and see the play," James said.

Amy sighed. "It isn't the same as being in it," she said unhappily. "But I'll cheer you all on, don't you worry."

Mandy bit her lip. Amy was trying hard to make the best of things. "How's Minnie?" she asked.

"Minnie is fine," said Amy. She looked at the white mouse running around its cage and tried to smile. "I thought maybe I

would bring her to see the play."

James giggled. "Just make sure she doesn't get out of her cage and run around," he said. "Can you imagine Mrs Ponsonby's face?"

Amy's smile got wider. "You bet I can," she said. "She'd be up on her chair, screeching the place down."

Mandy looked at Amy. Her eyes were dancing with mischief and she looked much more like her old self. If only she didn't have to miss out on being in the play.

But there was nothing they could do about that. *Or was there?* Sitting there, looking at Minnie running happily around in her cage, Mandy had an idea. She looked at her watch.

"Amy, we've got to go now," she said. "We're going to Hobart's Corner to see Mr Spellini."

James got up as well. "We'll see you tomorrow at school," he said.

"Or sooner," said Mandy and James

looked at her in surprise. Amy didn't seem to notice.

"What do you mean sooner?" James said as they walked down the front path of Amy's house.

Mandy hurried him on. "Come on," she said. "I've got something to ask Mr Spellini."

"What?" said James, running to keep up.

Mandy gave him a quick smile. "I know Amy can't be in the play," she said, "so we've just got to get Minnie into it instead!"

"But how will we manage to do that?" said James, running beside her.

"I don't know yet," said Mandy. "But we've got to try. I can't stand seeing Amy so unhappy, especially when she's trying so hard to make the best of it. That's why I want to see Mr Spellini."

James looked puzzled. "But what can he do?" he said.

Mandy shrugged and ran at the same time. "He's a magician, isn't he?" she said.

"He ought to be able to think of something."

Mr Spellini gave them a huge smile as they arrived, panting, at Hobart's Corner. He was feeding his doves and Jack was helping him.

"Look!" called Jack as they both came racing across the grass. "The doves are eating out of my hand."

"Jack likes to feed them so much they're going to get too fat to fly," Mr Spellini said, laughing.

"Whoops," said Jack. "Maybe I've given them enough."

"I think you have," said Mr Spellini, as Bianca fluttered up on to his shoulder.

"Let's put them back in their cage."

Jack, Mandy and James helped shut them in – while Bianca peered down at them from Mr Spellini's shoulder.

"How is she?" Mandy asked.

"She's terrific," the magician said. "I can't

thank your mother enough, Mandy. Bianca is totally recovered."

Mandy smiled back and looked at the pretty white dove. She certainly looked well.

"She's the nicest dove I've ever seen," Mandy said.

"She likes to sit on my shoulder," said Jack proudly. "Just the way she does with Mr Spellini."

Mr Spellini looked at Mandy and James closely.

"Something tells me you have something you want to talk to me about," he said.

James shook his head in wonder. "How did you know?" he said.

"Magic," said Mr Spellini. "And the way you came rushing into the garden."

"Oh, Mr Spellini, it's about Amy," Mandy said.

"That's the little girl who hurt her foot, isn't it?" said Mr Spellini.

Mandy nodded. "She's so upset that

she can't be in the play and neither can Minnie."

"Minnie?" said Mr Spellini, puzzled.

"Her white mouse," said James.

Mr Spellini rubbed his beard and looked thoughtful. "But what can I do?" he said.

"Well," said Mandy. "We thought that since you were a magician you might be able to do some magic for Amy."

"I can certainly do some tricks for her – to cheer her up," he said.

"Couldn't you magic her better?" asked Jack.

Mr Spellini smiled. "That's something magicians can't do, Jack," he said. "I only wish I could."

"I thought maybe you could think of some way of getting Minnie into the play," said Mandy.

Mr Spellini looked at Bianca. The dove ruffled her silky white feathers and put her head under her wing.

"I know how the little girl feels," Mr

Spellini said. "I was very upset when I thought I might not have Bianca in my act." He frowned. Then his face lit up. "James!" he said.

James looked up. "Yes?"

Mr Spellini smiled and his eyes began to twinkle. "How would you like to do a trick with a mouse?" he asked.

James blinked and shoved his glasses up on his nose.

"A trick with an animal?" he said. "But I've only done tricks with cards and ping pong balls and things."

Mr Spellini nodded. "I know," he said. "But you really are getting quite good." He looked at Mandy. "We shall have to give Mandy and Jack a special performance."

But Mandy wasn't listening. She was grinning with delight.

"You mean James could do a trick with Minnie? In the play?" she said.

"Perhaps," said Mr Spellini. "We'll have to work out a trick and see if it can be fitted into the story of the play."

Mandy bit her lip. "I hadn't thought of that," she said. "The play's finished and everybody knows their lines. We can't change it now."

"It isn't *quite* finished," James reminded her. "We still haven't decided what to do with Horrible Horace at the end."

Mandy swung round. "James, you're a genius!" she said. "That's it! That's the answer!"

"How?" said James.

Mandy's eyes sparkled. "Don't you see?" she said. "Horrible Horace has to learn his lesson. He's been so horrible to everyone because he's bigger than everybody else. He's a great big bully. So at the end of the play he should get a dose of his own medicine. He needs to know what it feels like to be small and helpless."

She looked at James and Mr Spellini. "You know, I think there is a part for Minnie in the play after all."

7

James the Magician

Mandy could hardly wait to tell Amy all about her idea. She rushed round to the Fentons' house straight after leaving Hobart's Corner. Amy was still in the garden. She was playing with Minnie, letting the little mouse run up and down her arm.

"I think she's feeling very left out," Mrs Fenton said as she and Mandy watched Amy from the kitchen window.

"Just wait till I tell her my idea, Mrs Fenton," Mandy said. "She'll feel better then, you'll see."

Mrs Fenton looked at her in surprise. "What idea?" she said.

Mandy smiled. "We've found a way to include Minnie in the play!" she said to Amy's mother.

"Minnie?" said Mrs Fenton. "But that would be wonderful." Then she smiled. "Come on," she said. "I think Amy should hear this first. Let's go and tell her."

Mandy ran out into the garden with Mrs Fenton following behind her. Amy looked up but she didn't smile. She was still really sad.

"Amy," said Mandy. "I've got a great surprise for you. Guess what? We've thought of a way to have Minnie in the play."

For a moment Amy didn't understand.

"Minnie?" she said. "What do you mean?"

Mandy sat down on the grass beside Amy and started to explain the plan. Gradually Amy's face cleared and lit up with excitement as she listened.

"That's terrific," she said when Mandy had finished. She looked down at Minnie, curled in her lap. "Do you hear that, Minnie?" she said. "You're going to be in

the play. You're going to be a star!"

Mandy grinned at Amy's happiness. "So can you come to Hobart's Corner tomorrow after tea?" she said. She turned to Mrs Fenton. "James is going to practise his tricks and Mr Spellini needs to see Minnie. We need a little box for her – for the trick."

"I'll bring Amy over," Mrs Fenton said. She looked at Amy and laughed. "I don't think I could stop her. I think she would hop all the way to Hobart's Corner if she had to."

Mandy grinned. Everything was working out.

James really did look the part the next evening at Hobart's Corner. The suns and moons on his cape glittered in the early evening sunlight and his pointy hat didn't fall off once during the whole practice. Underneath his cloak he had a white shirt with billowing sleeves, black trousers and black shiny boots. What a wizard!

The garden at Hobart's Corner was filled with people. Mr and Mrs Gardiner were there, plus the Hunters, Gran and Grandad, Amy, Mandy, Jack and Blackie. And, of course, James, Mr Spellini and Minnie. Mr Spellini's doves were perched in the apple tree.

James gave a great performance. First he did the trick with the ping pong ball, making it disappear right in front of Gran's eyes.

"Well, I never," said Gran. "How did you do that?"

Then he got Grandad to tear up a sheet of newspaper and place it in a wooden box. James tapped the box three times with his wand, then opened it – and there was a whole sheet of newspaper.

Grandad laughed. "Honestly," he said, "I watched every move you made and I can't work out how that was done."

"It's magic!" James said, taking a pack of

cards from his pocket. "Now I'm going to do a card trick."

He asked Mandy to pick a card and put it back in the pack. Then he shuffled the cards and picked out Mandy's card.

"How did you know which card I picked?" she said.

James looked mysterious. "I can't tell you that," he said. "I'm sworn to secrecy."

Mr Spellini nodded. "It wouldn't be magic if *everyone* could do it," he said.

Mandy smiled. James was so excited, his glasses kept sliding down his nose. He bit his lip in concentration, swirled round in his long black cloak and produced a bunch of flowers from nowhere. He presented the flowers to Mrs Gardiner.

"Oh, I wish I could grow flowers as easily as that," Gran said and everybody laughed.

"Do a trick for *me*," said Jack.

James fanned the pack of cards, got Jack to pick a card and put it back, then threw the pack up in the air. Jack watched the

cards fluttering down to earth. But Mandy had seen this trick before. She watched James. He took off his hat, tapped it with his magic wand – and Jack's card fell out!

"Wow!" said Jack.

"Bravo!" Mrs Gardiner shouted as James pulled a string of scarves from behind his left ear and gave them a final bow.

Mandy clapped loudly. "Your cloak looks great, Gran," she said.

"And your hat looks great too," said Gran.

Mandy was pleased. She had worked hard on that pointy hat! Everybody clapped enthusiastically. Blackie ran around the garden barking his head off, then came and leapt up on James, pawing at his cloak. The Labrador caught hold of something and tugged. It was a coloured flag.

"Blackie! No! Bad boy!" James shouted as Blackie tugged harder.

Then Blackie was off across the garden with a long trail of coloured flags flapping behind him. Mr Spellini's doves fluttered higher up into the apple tree.

"I reckon that's the end of the performance," Grandad said, laughing.

James raced after Blackie, his cloak fluttering in the breeze. His hat fell off as he ran. Mr Spellini picked it up and looked at it thoughtfully. Then he went over to his trunk and brought out a little box covered in silver paper. He turned to Amy.

"May I see Minnie?" he asked.

Amy took Minnie out of her cage and handed her to Mr Spellini. Mr Spellini took the little mouse carefully in his hands, clucking to her softly. Minnie twitched her whiskers. Then Mr Spellini hummed and rocked Minnie slowly in his hands. She blinked a few times and closed her eyes.

Mandy and Amy watched open-mouthed as Mr Spellini put Minnie gently into the silver box.

"Perfect," he said. "I hoped I would have something in my trunk that would do."

"You put her to sleep," Amy said, her eyes wide. "How did you do that?"

Mr Spellini looked at her and smiled. Mandy laughed.

"Don't tell us – magic!" she said as James came back with the coloured flags bunched in his hand.

"Sorry about that," he said, panting from the chase with Blackie.

Mr Spellini had his head in the trunk again. He brought out a thing that looked like a big black paper clip. "Just what I need," he said.

Mandy peeked into the trunk. It was full of weird-shaped objects and mirrors and boxes.

"Now, James," said Mr Spellini, "give me your hat and we'll start practising the mouse trick. I've thought of a way to do it."

Amy looked at the magician. "Minnie will be quite safe, won't she?" she asked nervously.

Mr Spellini stretched out a hand and at once a white dove swooped down from the apple tree and settled on his shoulder.

"It's Bianca!" Mandy said softly.

Mr Spellini tipped the dove gently on to Amy's shoulder. Bianca fluttered her feathers slightly then found her balance. She settled close to Amy's neck and made a soft bubbly sound deep in her throat.

"Oooh! That's lovely," said Amy, delighted.

Mr Spellini smiled. "You take care of Bianca and I shall take care of Minnie," he said. "Is it a deal?"

Amy stretched up a hand and stroked Bianca's feathers. "It's a deal," she said.

Mr Spellini looked thoughtful. "You know, James," he said, "I know you've got an apprentice. But every magician should have a proper assistant. What do you think? Would you like an assistant?"

James looked at Amy then he grinned at Mr Spellini.

"I think an assistant would be a great idea," he said.

Amy looked up at Mr Spellini. Her face broke into a wide smile.

"You mean me?" she said.

"You would feel better if you were James's assistant for the mouse trick," Mr Spellini said. "Then you could be sure that Minnie was all right."

"What would I have to do?" asked Amy.

"Just stand beside James," said Mr Spellini.

"Of course, you would need a costume."

"A costume!" Amy said. "I'd love a costume. But there isn't time, is there?"

Mandy put her head on one side. "We could ask Gran," she said. "She finished making my tunic for the play last night."

"Would she do it?" Amy asked.

"Why don't you go and see?" Mr Spellini said. "James and I have work to do."

"Oh, can't we stay and watch?" said Mandy.

But Mr Spellini shook his head.

"I know – magic secrets," Mandy said. But she didn't really mind.

"I want to go and ask about my costume," said Amy, pulling Mandy across the grass towards the house.

Mandy laughed. "You can hobble pretty fast when you want to, Amy," she said.

Amy turned a shining face to her. "I'm so excited," she said. "I really thought Minnie and I were going to be left out. Isn't it marvellous?"

Mandy nodded. "Just wait and see what Gran comes up with for a costume," she said. "That'll be marvellous too."

As they walked across the garden towards the house, Mandy looked back. James and Mr Spellini were bent over the pointy hat, examining it closely. What were they up to, she wondered.

8

Star of the show

"You look great!" Mandy said to Amy.

It was Saturday evening. Mandy and Amy were backstage waiting for the show to start. There were children everywhere. Those with pets had them safely secured in cages or travelling baskets.

"You look good, too. Your Gran is really

ace at making costumes," Amy said. "Nobody will guess what mine is made from."

Mandy nodded. There hadn't been much time to make anything complicated for Amy but Mrs Gardiner had found an old gold coloured curtain which she and Gran had made into a short swirly skirt with a little cape. Amy's hair was tied up with a big golden bow and she wore red boots to cover her bandage. She looked terrific.

Mandy, the wizard's apprentice, was wearing a bright green cap and a short red tunic over blue tights.

James was trying to stop Blackie jumping up at him.

"It's the wand," he said. "He wants me to throw it for him."

"That's because of his part in the play," Mandy said.

She took Blackie by the collar and hauled him off stage. She dug her hands deep into the pocket of her tunic and brought out a couple of dog treats.

"That's bribery," said Pam Stanton, walking past with Ginny the guinea-pig.

"It works," said Mandy as Blackie gobbled up the dog treats.

"There are thousands of people out there," Gary Roberts said, peering through a crack in the curtain. Gertie was draped round his neck.

Mandy came over and stood beside him. She gave Gertie a stroke. Then she saw the crowds.

"Wow!" she said. "The whole of Welford has turned up."

Gary laughed. "Look at Mrs Ponsonby," he said. "She's right in the front row."

Mandy looked. Mrs Ponsonby was sitting up straight in her chair, talking loudly to anybody who would listen.

"She's told the whole village that Mr Spellini is a dangerous spy," Jill Redfern said behind them.

Mandy turned round. Jill was giving Toto's shell a final polish.

"Doesn't he look lovely?" she said.

Mandy looked around. *Everybody* looked lovely. Gary had a big blue turban on his head, Amy sparkled and shone in her gold costume and James looked every inch a wizard with his tall hat, cloak and wand. Andrew was a proper villain, dressed up as Horace, all in black. He looked really sinister – a truly frightening giant!

Mrs Garvie clapped her hands softly. "Off the stage now," she said. "We're nearly ready to begin." She looked round at all her pupils. "What is it they say in the theatre? Break a leg!"

Amy looked down at her foot. "I nearly did that already," she said.

Everybody laughed and Mrs Garvie herded them off the stage. She put her fingers to her lips and pressed a button on the tape recorder at the side of the stage. At the same time the lights dimmed.

The music began and then the curtains slowly opened. The first batch of children ran on to the stage with their pets and the show began.

The group of children were acting as villagers at a carnival. There were all sorts of performers. There was dancing and singing and finally all the villagers did a conga round the stage.

Then Gary sat in the middle of the stage, holding Gertie up while Pam played the recorder backstage. Gary and Gertie were a great success. All the villagers cheered and brought their pets closer to see the fun.

But, as they gathered round Gary, a black figure appeared at the back of the stage. It was Horrible Horace. The villagers fell back in terror as Horace swept amongst them. He snatched Toto the tortoise from Jill and told the villagers what he wanted. If the villagers did not work for him and do everything he said, he would kill Toto – and all the animals in the village.

Horace marched to the front of the stage and glowered at the audience while, behind him, the villagers huddled together, wondering what to do.

Mandy, James and Susan were waiting in the wings.

"This is it," said James.

"I'm really nervous," Susan Davis said, putting on her monkey mask.

"You were great at rehearsal," James reassured her. He looked at Mandy. "Ready?"

Mandy nodded. "Good luck," she

whispered. She looked down at Blackie, standing beside Mrs Garvie. "It'll be your turn soon, Blackie," she said softly.

"You're on now," Mrs Garvie said, holding Blackie close to her side.

Mandy and James walked out on to the stage with Susan capering around them.

"Oh, Master," Mandy said in a clear voice. "This is a fine carnival. But nobody is having any fun. Why don't you show them some magic tricks?"

From then on, Mandy hardly had time to think. Everything worked perfectly. The villagers started having fun again. With the wizard's help, they all ganged up on Horace and tied him up. Pam played the recorder offstage while Gary swayed about so much his turban wobbled. Jack and Laura's rabbits received loud applause and each time Horrible Horace snarled and hissed, the audience booed and hissed back. Susan, the wizard's monkey, did her gymnastics, tumbling around the stage to terrific applause. But it was James and his magic tricks that got the loudest cheers. He was wonderful.

The play went so fast Mandy could hardly believe it when the last scene came.

Horrible Horace had escaped. He was standing centre stage and the villagers were cowering in front of him, afraid of him once again. He had stolen the wizard's magic wand and he was going to do something horrible to all the animals. The wizard lay helpless at Horrible Horace's feet. Without his wand, he had no power left. Horrible Horace lifted the wand up and waved it.

This was Blackie's cue. Mandy walked on from the wings with Blackie at her side.

"Look what you have done to my master!" she cried. "You have stolen his wand. You have stolen his power!"

Horace raised the wizard's magic wand higher.

"And now I'm going to turn all your pets to stone," he snarled.

Mandy knelt down centre stage, right next to James.

"Go, Blackie! Get Andrew!" she whispered to Blackie. "Fetch the stick!"

Blackie didn't need to be told twice. He made a dive for Horrible Horace and started chasing him round the stage. Horrible Horace threw the wand high into the air and Blackie leapt for it.

Mandy held her breath. Blackie caught the wand and turned to take it back to Andrew.

Mandy rattled the box of dog biscuits in her pocket and Blackie stopped and looked at her.

"Here, boy. Here, Blackie," she whispered.

Blackie put his head on one side and for a moment Mandy thought he wasn't going to come to her. Then he lolloped across the stage, put the wand down at Mandy's feet and wagged his tail.

"Good boy!" Mandy whispered and gave him a biscuit. There were laughs from the audience as he chomped it noisily.

Mandy put the wand into James's hand and stood up.

"Abracadabra, hubble and bubble, the wizard's wand will solve this trouble!" she said in a loud voice.

At once James leapt to his feet. The Wizard of Welford had got his power back. All the villagers cheered. Then they all went silent again as Horrible Horace started to walk towards James.

Mandy held her breath. Now it was time for the best trick of all. Amy was standing beside James. She had a small round object in her hand. Horrible Horace paced steadily towards James. Then James waved his wand three times. He twirled round, his cloak billowing behind him.

Just at that moment, Amy threw something down on the stage. There was a puff of smoke and Mandy saw Andrew dive off stage under cover of James's cloak and the smoke. James twirled again and swept his pointy hat off his head.

Mandy watched closely. She saw James reach inside the hat and there was the little silver box. In a moment he had the box open and held Minnie up for everyone to see. The Wizard of Welford had turned Horrible Horace into a mouse!

It was tremendous. The villagers on the stage cheered, the audience cheered. Amy looked as if she would turn a cartwheel in spite of her ankle. And, above them all, held in James's hand, was Minnie. The little mouse blinked in the bright lights and twitched her long whiskers.

All eyes were on the little mouse. She really was the star of the show.

"Horrible Horace will never bully the village again," James announced. "I have cast a spell on him – a spell to turn him into a tiny helpless little animal. The animals of Welford are safe!"

Then the curtain came down. They had to take five bows. Everybody was on their feet stamping and cheering. Finally Mrs Garvie had to come on and ask everyone to sit down.

"Mr Spellini is going to give us a very special treat," she said. "I think everybody knows how helpful he has been with the play."

There was clapping from the audience and Mrs Garvie held up her hand again until it died down.

"Mr Spellini has agreed to give a magic performance just for us," she said. She turned to the side of the stage and announced. "Ladies and Gentlemen, the Spectacular Spellini!"

Mandy, James and Amy sat down on the stage with all the other children. Everyone had their pets beside them, safely back in their baskets and cages. Blackie lay contentedly between Mandy and James, wagging his tail.

Mr Spellini began his act. He was amazing. He took three silver balls out of Pam Stanton's mouth. He turned Gary's turban into a beach ball. He made Andrew Pearson disappear entirely. He even smashed Mrs Garvie's watch with a big golden hammer – and gave it back to her without a mark on it.

"He's brilliant," said James. He grinned at Mandy. "He's the *real* Wizard of Welford."

"Oh, he's finished!" said Amy.

Mandy looked at the stage. Mr Spellini was bowing to the audience. Then he threw out his arms and his doves came fluttering down from the rafters above the stage. They settled along his outstretched arms, ruffling their feathers and cooing. Mandy spotted Bianca. The white dove walked up Mr Spellini's arm and settled in her favourite place on his shoulder.

The performance was over. It had all been wonderful. Mr Spellini turned to look at

Mandy. He gave her a wink and raised his
arms. The doves circled the stage above Mr
Spellini's head as he swept his hat off. He
took a huge bunch of flowers out of his
hat and threw them right over the stage
towards Mrs Ponsonby. Mrs Ponsonby was
so surprised, she threw up her hands with
a squeak of alarm – and caught them.

Mandy heard Mrs Ponsonby say,
"Well, really!"

Then she looked at the flowers. She
stood up and took a bow as well.

"Honestly, Mrs Ponsonby's got some cheek," said James.

"Who cares?" said Amy softly, stroking the little mouse. "Minnie is a star. It's magic!"

Mandy nodded happily. "Magic," she repeated. Then she looked at Minnie. "It's mouse magic!"

Animal Ark Pets™

Chick Challenge

Chick Challenge
Special thanks to Helen Magee

Text copyright © 1996 Working Partners Ltd.
Original series created by Ben M. Baglio, London W6 0QT
Illustrations copyright © 1996 Paul Howard

First published as a single volume in Great Britain in 1997
by Hodder Children's Books

Contents

1

A new arrival

"I'm *so* excited about Duchess's kittens," Mandy Hope said to James Hunter as they walked along Welford's main street to school.

James smiled. "You get excited about all the animals that come to Animal Ark," he said.

Mandy's parents were both vets in Welford. Their surgery was at the back of Animal Ark, the stone cottage where Mandy and her parents lived.

"But it's *always* exciting," Mandy said. "I think it must be much more interesting looking after animals than people. I mean, people are all the same. Animals are all different."

"Like four-legged ones and two-legged ones," said James.

"And some with no legs at all," said Mandy. "Like Gertie, Gary's garter-snake."

Gary Roberts was in Mandy's class at Welford Primary School. He had a pet garter-snake. Mandy always took a great interest in the pets of her school-friends.

"Duchess was in for a check-up yesterday," she said. "Her kittens are due any time now."

Duchess was Richard Tanner's Persian cat and this was her very first litter. Richard was also in Mandy's class.

James hitched his schoolbag on to his

shoulder. "You'd rather have animals than people any day, Mandy," he said.

Mandy grinned. She loved going home every day to find out what new animals had arrived at Animal Ark.

"Dad says that too," she said. "In fact, so does Mum!"

"So does *everybody*!" said James.

Mandy laughed. James was her best friend. He was in the class below her at school – and he liked animals almost as much as she did. "You can talk!" she said.

"So," said Mrs Todd at the end of afternoon school. "You've all got to think about what we're going to do at Easter. Let's have your ideas. You've usually got plenty." She looked at Mandy. "Oh, Mandy, Mrs Garvie wants to see you. You can go along now."

"Me?" said Mandy, surprised. Mrs Garvie was the Headteacher of Welford Primary School.

"Don't worry," said Mrs Todd. "There's something she wants you to help her with. You aren't in any trouble."

The Headteacher's door was open when Mandy arrived. Mrs Garvie turned to her and smiled. There was a little girl standing beside her. She had dark curly hair and looked about five years old.

"Come in, Mandy," Mrs Garvie said. She looked at the little girl. "This is Libby Masters," she went on. "She lives at Blackheath Farm up on the moor and

she's had to start school late in the term. I'd like you to look after her for me."

Mandy looked at Libby and smiled. "Of course I will," she said to Mrs Garvie.

Mrs Garvie smiled at Libby. "I told you we could rely on Mandy," she said. "I'm sure she'll take good care of you." Then she turned to Mandy again. "Libby's mum is coming to collect her soon," she said. "Why don't you get to know each other in the meantime?"

Mandy nodded. "Let's go and find James," she said to Libby. "You'll like him. He's got a black Labrador called Blackie and a cat called Benji. Do you like animals?"

Libby nodded, but Mandy could see her bottom lip trembling as she followed Mandy out of the Headteacher's room.

"Do you have any pets?" she asked gently.

"You mean, like a dog or a cat?" said Libby. She shook her head.

"Never mind," said Mandy. "You live

on a farm, so there must be lots of animals around. You don't need to have a pet of your own."

The bell for end of school rang as they came out into the playground.

"Do *you* have a pet?" Libby asked.

Mandy smiled and shook her head. "I'm like you," she said. "My mum and dad are vets so there are always lots of animals around, but I don't have a special pet of my own."

"Hi! Mandy!" called a voice.

Mandy looked up. "There's James," she said.

James ran up to them, his face flushed. "Have you heard about the fancy dress party?" he asked.

Mandy shook her head.

James grinned. "It was Laura Baker's idea," he said. "Mrs Black was talking about what we would do for Easter. We had a picnic last year, remember?"

"I like rolling eggs at Easter," Libby said.

Mandy gave Libby a quick look. She looked a lot more cheerful.

"This is Libby Masters, James," she said. "I told Mrs Garvie we'd look after her for a few days. She just started school today."

James grinned at Libby. "What was your last school like?" he said.

Libby bit her lip. "I didn't go to school," she said. "I couldn't start. I had a broken leg."

James looked sympathetic. "That was rotten luck," he said. "It isn't easy starting late, is it?"

Libby looked grateful. "Oh, no," she said. "It's really hard."

"Was your leg very sore?" Mandy asked.

Libby shook her head. "Only at first," she said. "But I couldn't run about."

"You must have been lonely," Mandy said.

Libby nodded and her eyes lit up for a moment. "I had Ronda," she said.

Mandy was just going to ask who Ronda was when Laura Baker came running up.

"Did James tell you about the Easter party?" she said to Mandy. "It's fancy dress. Jack Gardiner and I are going to go as Easter bunnies. We're going to make bunny masks with big front teeth and huge ears. What will you go as, Mandy?"

Mandy laughed. "I've only just heard about it!" she said.

"Isn't it great that Jack and I both have rabbits?" Laura said. "Mrs Black says we can bring them with us to the party."

James's face lit up. "Does that mean I can take Blackie?" he said.

"Blackie would love to come," said Mandy.

"You could make him an Easter bonnet," Laura said, giggling.

"I don't think Blackie would like that very much," James said.

"You'll really enjoy the Easter party, Libby," Mandy said to the little girl.

"What kind of mask are you going to make?" Laura asked Libby.

"Libby hasn't got a pet," said Mandy, "so she could choose any kind of mask – like me."

"You could come as a rabbit, with Jack and me," Laura said. "I've got three of them – Nibbles, Patch and Fluffy. You could carry Patch if you like. He's very friendly and rabbits are really Eastery."

James grinned. "*Eastery*," he said. "I like that. What else is Eastery?"

"Chickens," Mandy said. "Little Easter chicks."

James looked at Libby. "There you are then, Libby," he said. "You and Mandy could go as Easter chickens. You could make chick masks."

Mandy turned eagerly to Libby. The little girl's eyes were fixed on James. Suddenly her bottom lip began to tremble

and her eyes filled with tears. Mandy reached out a hand to her but she turned away. Libby ran across the playground to the school gate. Mandy watched as a car drew up and a woman got out. Libby ran right into her arms.

"Wow!" said James. "What did I say?"

Mandy frowned, her eyes on the car as it drew away from the school gates. "I don't know, James," she said. "I'm sure you didn't say anything to upset her."

James shoved his glasses up his nose. "I

hope not," he said. "Poor kid. She really does seem unhappy, doesn't she?"

Mandy nodded. "Yes, she does," she said. "And I wish I knew why."

2

Who is Ronda?

Mandy waited patiently at the school
gate next morning. She wanted to be
there when Libby's mum dropped her
off. When the car drew up, Libby
gave her a big smile and Mandy
relaxed. This morning the little girl
seemed fine.

Libby's mum got out and came to the gate with her daughter. Mandy smiled up at her.

"You must be Mandy," Mrs Masters said. "Libby has told me all about you – and your friend James. You've been really kind to Libby."

Mandy blushed. "It's really hard to start school late," she said.

Mrs Masters nodded. "I know," she said. "Everybody has made friends already. I think Libby feels a little left out. It's a pity. We were really looking forward to Libby making lots of friends at school. Our farm is so isolated. She hardly ever sees other children."

Mandy looked at Libby and smiled. "You'll soon have lots of friends, Libby. You'll see," she said.

Mrs Masters gave Libby a quick hug and drove off. Mandy and Libby walked through the school gates together.

"Don't you have anybody at all to play with at home?" asked Mandy.

Libby thought for a moment. "I've got Ronda," she said.

"What's Ronda like?" Mandy said, interested.

Libby's head drooped. "She's got a lovely red coat," she said and her mouth turned down.

Mandy changed the subject. It seemed that thinking about her friend, Ronda, made the little girl sad. If only she knew why.

She and James puzzled over Ronda during the rest of the week.

"I wonder what it is about Ronda that makes her so sad," Mandy said on their way home from school on Wednesday.

"Ask her," said James.

Mandy shook her head. "I don't want to upset Libby," she said. "I mean, maybe her friend is moving away or maybe she's ill. But every time she mentions Ronda she nearly starts to cry."

James nodded. "I know what you

mean," he said. "I asked her what Ronda's favourite lunch was."

"And?" said Mandy.

James grinned. "Would you believe cornflakes?" he answered. "At least, I think that's what Libby said. She looked as if she was going to burst into tears so I didn't ask any more."

"I'm sure that Ronda is at the bottom of Libby's unhappiness," said Mandy.

"But if we can't ask Libby, how do we find out about Ronda? I've never heard of anybody called Ronda in Welford."

Mandy sighed. "Neither have I," she said. "And neither has Mum or Dad. I asked them."

James frowned. "What about your gran?" he said. "She knows everybody."

Mandy looked at James and smiled. "Brilliant!" she said. "If Gran doesn't know who Ronda is, then nobody does. Let's go round and see her after tea."

"I'll take Blackie," said James. "He loves going to Lilac Cottage."

Mandy giggled. "You mean he loves the fruit bushes!" she said.

James looked embarrassed. "Maybe I should leave him behind," he said.

"Oh, no, don't do that," said Mandy. "Gran and Grandad love Blackie."

"Get out of my raspberry canes, you young whippersnapper!" Grandad said, collaring Blackie.

James raised his eyebrows and looked at Mandy. But Mandy was laughing at Grandad and Blackie.

"Blackie knows you don't mean it," she said to her grandad.

Grandad grinned at her as Blackie put his front paws on his chest and started licking his face.

"Talk about soft," said Gran from the kitchen door. "Come on, Blackie, come and get a biscuit."

He gave a short bark and dashed into the kitchen after Gran.

"Cupboard love," said Grandad

brushing down his jumper. He looked at
Mandy and James. "How about a cool
drink?" he suggested.

Mandy and James nodded. "Grandad,
have you ever heard of a little girl called
Ronda?" Mandy asked.

"In Welford?" said Grandad.

Mandy shrugged. "I suppose she
might live on one of the farms up on
the moors," Mandy said.

"Maybe near where the Masters' farm
is," James added.

"The Masters?" said Gran as they came into the kitchen. "They have a free-range poultry farm up at Blackheath. How is little Libby getting on at school?"

Mandy frowned. "She seems really unhappy," she said, sitting down at the table.

Gran poured two glasses of orange juice for Mandy and James, and put a plate of home-made biscuits in front of them.

"We think it's got something to do with her friend, Ronda," said James.

"I don't think I know any Rondas," said Gran. "Where does she live?"

Mandy sighed. "We don't know," she said. "We thought if anybody would know, *you* would."

"Maybe Ronda is her sister," said Grandad.

Gran shook her head. "Libby is an only child," she said.

"Every time we ask Libby about Ronda she gets upset," said James. "If we knew what was upsetting her, maybe we could help."

Gran nodded. "I see," she said. "Of course it must be very lonely for Libby up on that farm. There isn't another house anywhere near it."

"So if she had a friend, it would be even more important to her," said Mandy.

"And if her friend was sick – or maybe moving away – then she would be really upset," said James.

"But you can't really begin to help until you know who Ronda is," said Grandad.

Mandy and James nodded.

"You leave it to me," Gran said. "I'll make enquiries."

"What do you know about this Ronda?" Grandad asked.

"Nothing much," said Mandy. "We know she wears a red coat . . ."

"And she likes cornflakes," said James.

Gran and Grandad looked at them blankly.

"Well!" said Gran. "That's *something* to

go on, I suppose."

"How about asking Mrs McFarlane?" Grandad suggested. "She knows everybody."

Mr and Mrs McFarlane ran the post office in Welford. The post office was Mandy and James's favourite shop.

"Good idea," said James. "We'll pop in tomorrow on the way to school."

"And I'll start asking everyone at the WI," said Gran. She was chairwoman of Welford Women's Institute.

"Don't you worry," said Grandad. "We'll soon find out who this Ronda is!"

But by the end of the week, Ronda was still a mystery.

"Even Mrs McFarlane has never heard of her," Mandy said to her parents as she sat at the kitchen table, her homework spread out in front of her.

Mrs Hope pulled out a chair and sat down at the table beside Mandy. "You know," she said, "I've been thinking about this Ronda. Maybe she doesn't exist after all."

"But Libby talked about her. She's her friend," said Mandy.

Mrs Hope nodded sympathetically. "I know," she said. "But from what you've told me Libby seems to be quite lonely up on that farm. There aren't any other children about and she has no brothers and sisters."

Mr Hope frowned. "But what about Ronda?" he said, his dark eyes puzzled.

Mrs Hope pushed a curl of red hair back from her forehead. "Maybe there isn't any Ronda," she said. "Maybe she is an imaginary friend."

Mandy opened her mouth and looked at her mum. "Imaginary!" she said.

Emily Hope nodded. "Lonely children often have make-believe friends," she said. "Nobody else can see them, but they're very real to the child. And with Libby being an only child . . ."

"I'm an only child," said Mandy. "I

never had an imaginary friend."

Mr Hope smiled and his eyes twinkled. "Every patient that's passed through Animal Ark has been your friend, Mandy," he said. "You've never needed to make one up!"

Mandy grinned back. "I suppose so," she said. She thought for a moment. "So why does she get so upset when she talks about Ronda?" she asked.

Mrs Hope frowned. "I don't know. Maybe going to school has made her realise that Ronda isn't real. Maybe she doesn't want to let her pretend friend go."

Mandy thought hard. "I can see that," she said. "But I don't see how we can help Libby." She shook her head. "An imaginary friend. I never thought of that!"

3

Duchess in trouble

"That explains the red coat and eating cornflakes for lunch anyway," James said next day coming home from school. "I mean, imaginary friends don't have to act like real people."

"So what do we do?" asked Mandy.

James shrugged. "We can be Libby's

friends," he said. "At least until she gets over her shyness. Then she'll probably make friends with people in her own class."

"Maybe I could ask her to tea at Animal Ark," said Mandy.

"That's a good idea," James said. "You could show her some of the animals your mum and dad are looking after."

"I'll bet Libby would love to have a pet of her own," Mandy said. "What kind do you think she would like?"

As Mandy and James came into the reception at Animal Ark, Jean Knox looked up from her desk.

"Your mum is out on a call and your dad is in the operating room," she said.

Jean Knox was Animal Ark's receptionist. She sounded worried. Jean's glasses were dangling round her neck on their chain as usual, but her normally cheerful face looked strained.

"What's wrong, Jean?" Mandy said. "Is it an emergency?"

Jean nodded, her eyes serious. "It's Duchess," she said. "She got knocked down this afternoon."

Mandy and James looked at Jean in horror. "But Duchess is expecting her kittens any day now," Mandy said. "Is she badly hurt?"

"Her leg looked quite bad when Mrs Tanner brought her in," Jean said. "Your dad thought the shock might bring on the birth. So poor Duchess has got that to cope with too. Simon is

in there as well. They'll do everything they can."

Simon was the practice nurse – and a very good one.

"Does Richard know?" asked James.

"Mrs Tanner has gone home to tell him when he comes in from school," Jean said. "She said they'd be right back."

Mandy nodded. "Is there anything I can do, Jean?" she asked.

Jean looked out of the window behind her. "You could put the kettle on for a cup of tea, Mandy," she said. "That always helps. Oh, here come Richard and his mum now."

Mandy nodded and went into the kitchen to put the kettle on. James followed her.

"Poor Richard," he said. He unhooked some blue and white mugs from the kitchen dresser and put them on the worktop.

"Poor *Duchess*," Mandy said. "And what's going to happen to her kittens?"

"Your dad will do his very best," James said reassuringly.

Mandy nodded. "I know that," she said. "Oh, I wish I knew what was happening in the operating room."

The kettle boiled. Mandy poured the water carefully into the teapot and set it on the tray.

"Come on," she said. "Let's go and keep Richard and his mum company while they're waiting."

Richard was sitting beside his mother in the reception area. He looked really pale and Mandy thought he was only just managing to hold back the tears.

"I'll never forgive myself," Mrs Tanner said to Jean. "I don't know how I managed to leave the door open. It was only for a minute."

Mandy put the teapot on a low table and James set down the tray.

"Tea," said Jean briskly as she came round the desk.

Mrs Tanner accepted a cup gratefully. Richard looked as if he hadn't even heard Jean.

"What hit Duchess?" James asked.

Mrs Tanner bit her lip. "A car," she said. "The driver was very apologetic but he said he expected Duchess to move faster than she did. He said he did his best to avoid her."

Mandy had a sudden vision of Duchess stalking across the road in her usual stately manner – except that, being pregnant with her kittens, she would be too heavy to make a dash for safety.

Richard just sat there, staring in front of him, his eyes dark with misery.

The operating-room door opened and they all turned towards it. Mandy could hear her heart beating as she forced herself to look at her dad's face.

"Richard," Mr Hope said softly.

Mandy could hardly breathe. Surely it wouldn't be bad news. Then she saw that her dad was smiling. He ran a hand through his thick hair and shook his head slightly.

"You've got quite a lady there," he said to Richard. "Duchess is now the proud mother of three kittens and, apart from her leg, I reckon she's going to be all right."

Mandy's heart was thumping so loudly she could hardly take in what her dad was saying. Duchess wasn't dead. Duchess was going to be all right. And three kittens!

"It's going to be a while before she's on her feet," Mr Hope continued. "And I'm afraid she might have a limp."

Richard's face brightened. "And her kittens," he said. "Are they OK?"

Mr Hope frowned. "We couldn't save two, I'm afraid, but the others look fine," he said. "Duchess is still pretty uncomfortable, so I think I'll keep her here until we see how she's managing."

"Can I see her?" Richard asked.

Mr Hope smiled. "Just for a moment,"

he said. "Simon is with her."

Richard disappeared into the operating room.

"Is she really going to be all right?" Mrs Tanner asked quietly.

Mr Hope nodded. "She'll need a lot of tender loving care for a while. Looking after the kittens might be difficult for her. But she should be as good as new in a couple of months' time – except for a bit of a limp."

"Oh, she'll get all the tender loving and care we can give her," Mrs Tanner said.

"Now I'd better get her into the residential unit," Mr Hope said.

"Can we come?" said Mandy. "Can we see the kittens?"

"As if I could stop you!" said Mr Hope. "Come on then. But don't disturb her, she's very sleepy."

Richard turned as they came into the operating room. "Look!" he called quietly. "Look at Duchess and her kittens."

Mandy and James came to stand beside him. Simon was just finishing bandaging Duchess's leg. But Duchess wasn't paying too much attention to that. Instead she was licking the little bodies curled up against her, all her concentration on her kittens.

Mandy looked at the tiny, sightless little bundles of fur. "Oh, Duchess," she said. "They're beautiful."

"Well, well," said Mr Hope. "It looks as if Duchess is going to make a fine

mother." He scratched his head. "In fact, it just might be the best thing for her at the moment."

"What do you mean?" Mandy asked.

Mr Hope pointed to Duchess. "Look at her," he said. "She's so taken up with her kittens she doesn't seem to notice her leg is injured. I reckon she'll get better all the quicker with her little family to take her mind off her injuries."

Mandy smiled. "Of course she will," she said. "They're such beautiful babies!"

Mandy was so busy for the next few days, looking in on Duchess and the kittens and reporting back to Richard, that she almost forgot she had planned to ask Libby over for tea. It was only when her mum got a call from the Masters' farm that she remembered.

"Some of Mr Masters' hens are sick," Mrs Hope said as she put the phone down. "I'm going to take some vaccine up there. How would you like to come and see Libby, Mandy?"

"Could I?" said Mandy, turning away from Duchess. The kittens were getting stronger by the day.

"We can bring her back for tea if you like," Mrs Hope said. "I know you wanted to ask her."

Mandy blushed. "I forgot."

"Come on then," said Mrs Hope. "Get your wellies. If we're going to visit a poultry farm you'll need them."

The Masters' farm was high up on the moor. The whole of Welford was spread out below them as the Land-rover bumped its way along the farm track. Mandy looked up at the scudding clouds. The wind was fresh and strong, and the clouds made shadows on the hills. The Masters must get cut off in winter sometimes, she thought.

"I'm not surprised Libby invented a friend," Mandy said. "It must be lonely for her up here."

"It'll be nice for her to have a visitor

this afternoon," Mrs Hope said.

"There she is," said Mandy as they turned into the farmyard.

Libby was standing with her dad, waiting for Mrs Hope.

"Hi, Libby," said Mandy jumping down from the Land-rover as it stopped.

Libby's face broke into a pleased smile. "Mandy!" she said. She looked suddenly shy. "Would you like to see Ronda?"

Mandy's mouth dropped open in surprise. "See her?" she said.

Libby nodded.

Mandy looked at her mum. How on earth would she be able to "see" an imaginary friend? Maybe she would just have to pretend.

Mrs Hope looked just as surprised as Mandy felt.

"Oh, Ronda is a beauty," Mr Masters said. "You must see her. Come along."

Mandy and Mrs Hope watched as Mr Masters marched off across the farmyard with Libby skipping at his side.

"What do we do?" Mandy asked her mother.

Mrs Hope shrugged. "If Mr Masters can pretend to see Ronda, then so can we," she said. "Just do what he does."

Mandy and Mrs Hope rounded the corner of the barn and found Libby and her dad leaning over a wire enclosure.

"There she is," said Libby, looking in.

Mandy looked. There were about a dozen chickens in the enclosure and that was all. No little girl – no friend.

Libby opened a gate and made a chirruping sound. "Come on, Ronda," she said. "Come and meet Mandy."

Mandy looked in disbelief as a large hen with beautiful russet feathers strutted towards them. She marched through the gate and right up to Libby.

"Didn't I tell you she was a beauty?" Mr Masters said.

Libby looked at the hen proudly. "This is Ronda," she said to Mandy. "Isn't she

just beautiful? Look at her wonderful red feathers."

Mandy watched as the little girl put her hand in her pocket and brought out some corn.

"This is her favourite," Libby said. "Ronda just loves corn."

Ronda pecked up the corn. Then she stuck her head in Libby's pocket, looking for more.

"Ronda!" Libby giggled. "That tickles. Come and do your dance for Mandy."

Libby stood up and let a stream of corn fall from her hand. Ronda picked her way delicately amongst it, pecking it up, following the trail as the little girl made circles of corn on the ground.

Mandy looked at Ronda. The red coat. The corn. That was the mystery explained. Ronda was a hen. And not just an ordinary hen – a dancing one!

4

The amazing dancing hen

"You should put her on the stage," said Mandy. "She's terrific!"

"She's a Rhode Island Red," Libby said proudly, scattering the rest of the corn for Ronda.

"She's more like a member of the family than a hen," said Mr Masters. He laughed.

"Sometimes she comes into the house to watch TV. She just settles herself down beside Libby. You'd think she understood every word."

Mrs Hope smiled. "Rhode Island Reds make great pets," she said. "They often get really attached to a family."

Mr Masters scratched his head. "Ronda is certainly attached to Libby," he said. "When she was ill Ronda used to come and sit beside her. She was great company for her."

"She follows me around everywhere," said Libby. Then her face fell. "Only she hates me going to school. She misses me – and I miss her."

"Maybe you could have a look at Ronda while you're here, Mrs Hope," Mr Masters said. "She doesn't seem to be ill, but I don't mind telling you I've been quite worried about her recently. She hasn't been laying well at all and I don't think her coat is as healthy as it should be."

Mrs Hope bent down and gathered Ronda gently into her hands, turning the hen round and examining her.

"Her feathers *are* a bit dull," said Mrs Hope. "Nothing to worry about yet. Is she eating?"

Libby shook her head. "Sometimes she doesn't eat at all when I'm not here."

"That could be serious," said Mrs Hope. "If she doesn't eat properly she'll stop laying altogether." She looked at Libby. "I think Ronda is pining for you,"

she said. "Missing you while you're at school."

"Does that mean she'll get sick?" Libby asked.

Mrs Hope smiled reassuringly, but she looked concerned. "Maybe," she said. "So what we have to do is find some way of stopping her pining and that will stop her getting sick."

"How?" said Libby. "Mummy says I have to go to school – and I can't take Ronda."

"No," said Mrs Hope. "It's a problem, Libby."

Mandy looked at her mother. What on earth could they do? Libby was unhappy because she had to leave Ronda at home. Ronda was pining because she missed Libby. If Ronda got sick, Libby would be even more unhappy.

"Is there anything you can do for her at the moment?" Mr Masters asked Mrs Hope.

Mrs Hope looked thoughtful. "I can

give you some vitamin supplements to put in her feed," she said. "It would probably be a good idea to make sure she got some extra protein as well. But what she really needs is something to fill the gap that Libby leaves when she goes to school."

"You mean, like something to interest her," said Mandy.

"Something to stop her missing Libby," said Mr Masters. He looked at Mandy and Libby. "That *is* a puzzle," he said. "I'll have to think about that . . . but meanwhile I should see to my other hens."

Mandy and Libby watched as Mrs Hope and Mr Masters made their way across the farmyard to the henhouses.

"If Ronda stops eating, she'll die," Libby said to Mandy.

Mandy put out a hand and stroked the hen's coat gently. Ronda ruffled her feathers and settled close to Libby's chest.

"We won't let that happen, Libby,"

Mandy said. "We'll think of something."

Libby looked at Mandy. "Promise?"

Mandy looked at the little girl with her hen cradled in her arms. "I promise."

Mandy was very quiet all the way home.

"You're worrying about Ronda, aren't you?" her mum said as they turned into the driveway at Animal Ark.

Mandy nodded. "I didn't know hens could get so attached to somebody," she said.

Mrs Hope smiled. "It isn't just dogs and cats that get fond of people," she said. "All kinds of animals miss their owners and start to mope. Rhode Island Reds are famous for becoming part of the family."

Mandy bit her lip. "I promised Libby I would think of something," she said.

"Meantime you've got to say goodbye to your favourite patients," Mrs Hope said, getting out of the Land-rover. "Richard and his mother are coming to collect Duchess and the kittens tonight."

Mandy smiled. "I won't mind really," she said. "Duchess will be much happier at home with Richard."

"Even though she has been in the best animal hotel in Welford," Mrs Hope said.

Mandy grinned. "The very best!"

Mr Hope gave Duchess and the kittens a final check before Richard took them home.

Mandy cuddled the Persian cat gently. "No more running out of the door, Duchess," she said, trying to sound severe. "You're a grown-up mum now. You've got to give a good example to your kittens."

Duchess just yawned.

"I don't think Duchess will be running around much for a while," said James. "She'll be far too busy looking after her babies. She won't want to let them out of her sight."

James and Mandy watched as Richard

walked off down the path. He had the kittens safely tucked up in a carrying basket, while his mother carried Duchess in a separate box.

"That reminds me," said Mandy. "I've found out who Ronda is."

James listened open-mouthed while Mandy told him all about the hen.

"Poor Libby," James said when Mandy had finished. "It must be rotten for her going off to school every day, knowing that Ronda will be pining."

"What Ronda needs is something to hold her attention," Mandy said. "Something to stop her missing Libby."

James thought for a moment. "Chicks!" he said.

"What?" said Mandy.

James turned to her, his eyes gleaming with excitement. "Chicks," he said again. "If Ronda had chicks to look after, she wouldn't have time to miss Libby. Look at Duchess and her kittens! She hardly even notices her sore leg."

Mandy looked at him in delight. "James, you're brilliant!" she said. Then her face fell. "No, that won't work."

"Why not?" asked James.

Mandy shook her head. "For chicks you need eggs," she replied. "And Mr Masters is afraid that Ronda is going to stop laying,"

"Oh," said James. "That is a problem."

Mandy looked at him. "Let's go and ask Dad," she said. "There must be something we can do. It's *such* a good idea, James."

"They don't have to be Ronda's eggs," said Mr Hope. "Just as long as the eggs are fertile, Ronda can sit on them and hatch out chicks. Then the chicks will belong to Ronda."

"What do you mean, fertile?" asked Mandy.

"Some eggs will hatch into chicks – they're the fertile ones," Mr Hope explained. "Others don't hatch into chicks. They're called infertile. They're the eggs we eat for breakfast."

Mandy and James looked at each other in delight.

"There's only one problem," Mrs Hope said.

Mandy and James looked at her.

"Ronda wasn't broody when I saw her," she said.

"What does *that* mean?" James asked.

Mrs Hope smiled. "If a hen is going to hatch out eggs it has to be broody," she said. "That means it has to want to sit on its nest. Hatching eggs takes a long time – three whole weeks. You can't force a hen to sit on eggs."

"So it won't work," said Mandy.

"I wouldn't say that," Mr Hope said. "There are ways of encouraging a hen to turn broody, and Rhode Island Reds make very good broodies."

"What sorts of ways?" asked Mandy.

"Like putting china eggs in its nest," said Mr Hope. "You can sometimes persuade a hen to sit on china eggs, then replace them with real ones once the hen has decided to sit on them."

"But how would we persuade Ronda to sit on the china eggs?" Mandy said.

"Ah, that might take a bit of patience," said Mr Hope.

"And a bit of luck," added Mrs Hope.

Mandy and James looked at each other. Mandy lifted her chin. "It's worth a try," she said.

James grinned at her.

"Uh-oh," he said. "I know that look! Poor Ronda doesn't stand a chance. She'll be sitting on her eggs in no time at all."

5

A difficult task

"So what we've got to do is try to make Ronda want to sit on her nest," Mandy said to Libby next day at school.

"Do you think your dad has any china eggs?" James asked.

Libby nodded. "Oh, yes," she said. "I've seen what he does with them."

"Does it really work?" said Mandy.

Libby frowned. "Yes," she said. "But he only ever does it with hens that have already started sitting on their nest."

"You mean they've *gone* broody," said James.

Libby nodded again. "I don't see how we can get Ronda to do that," the little girl said. "She always wants to follow me around."

"Then you'll just have to sit on the nest with her," James joked.

Libby looked at him in surprise and smiled. "I never thought of that," she said.

"James was joking," Mandy said.

Libby giggled. "I know," she said. "I'd be a bit big for a nest!"

Mandy and James laughed.

"Why don't we come up to the farm tomorrow," Mandy suggested. "I know Dad is coming up to see if the vaccine worked."

Libby nodded. "That would be great! And I'll ask Dad about the china eggs."

"I don't know about this," Mr Masters said next day. "Libby has made a special nest for Ronda in the broody pen by the barn. There are a few broodies there already, but Ronda doesn't look as if she wants to sit on the nest."

"Let's go and see if we can help," Mandy said to James.

"Good luck!" Mr Hope said as he and Mr Masters went off towards the big hen pen.

Mandy and James found Libby trying to coax Ronda on to her nesting-box. Ronda strutted around the scratching area.

"Come on, Ronda," Libby said softly. She looked round as Mandy and James appeared. Then she put her fingers to her lips. "Shh," she said. "We have to be quiet or we'll disturb the other nesting birds."

Mandy looked in the nesting-box. It was tucked neatly under the low roof of the pen and lined with straw.

"Why is it up there?" whispered James.

"The nesting-box has to be off the ground," said Libby. "It's to keep the eggs safe from any rats or foxes that might get into the pen."

Poor Libby didn't look very happy. "Dad says if Ronda doesn't start to sit soon she'll have to come out of the broody pen," she said. "He thinks she'll put the other broodies off. All their chicks are due next week."

Mandy looked along the length of the pen. There were flutterings from all the other nesting-boxes and the soft sound of hens clucking to themselves in the warm darkness of the nests. It was very peaceful.

"Do they stay there all the time?" James said.

Libby nodded. "They come out for a scratch-around every day," she said. "But only for about fifteen minutes. The eggs would get cold if the hens left the nest for longer than that."

"How long do they stay there?" asked Mandy.

"Three weeks," Libby said. She smiled. "Can you imagine sitting in the same place for three weeks? No wonder Ronda doesn't want to do it."

Mandy looked at the Rhode Island Red. "But it's natural for hens to sit on their eggs," she said.

"I know she would just love chicks," Libby said. "She'd make a wonderful mother."

"Have you tried lifting her on to the nest?" James wondered.

Libby nodded. "But I'll try again," she said. "You never know."

Mandy and James watched as Libby carefully slid her hands under Ronda's body and lifted the hen into her arms. Ronda ruffled her feathers and settled down in the little girl's arms. Libby carried her over to the nest and placed her there. Ronda settled down and began to peck at the straw in the nest, making soft burbling noises.

Mandy and James stood watching silently. Ronda fluttered again and settled deeper into the straw.

Libby rose and Ronda looked round sharply, ready to move and follow her mistress.

"Maybe if you stayed with her for a little while," Mandy suggested.

Libby looked at Ronda. "When I put her on before she just got off again," she said. "Do you think she'll stay this time?"

"She might," said Mandy. "If she gets really comfortable."

"I'll stay with her for a while," Libby said. "Can you and James get the china eggs from Mum? Then we'll be ready if she decides to sit."

Mandy and James slipped quietly out of the broody pen. They didn't want to alarm Ronda. Mandy looked back: Ronda was sitting quietly on the nest and Libby was standing beside her in the darkness. Just as she turned to go Mandy heard Ronda make a low, contented clucking sound. Maybe their plan was going to work after all.

Mr Hope came out of the farmhouse with Mr and Mrs Masters. He was ready to go, but Mandy and James were really reluctant to leave just yet. Mrs Masters had two big brown eggs in her hand.

"These are for you," she said to Mandy and James.

They looked at them with interest. Then Mandy realised what they were.

"They're the china eggs," she said. "But they look just like real ones."

Mr Masters chuckled. "That's the idea," he said. "They have to be good if they're going to fool a hen."

"How is it going down there?" Mrs Masters asked.

Mandy and James looked at each other.

"Ronda was sitting on the nest when we left," said Mandy.

"Libby is with her," James added.

Mr Masters shook his head. "You

have to be sure she's going to sit tight before you put any fertile eggs under her," he said.

"How long before you can be sure?" James asked.

Mr Masters scratched his chin. "If she's still there in the morning, we might risk it at dusk tomorrow," he said.

"Why dusk?" said Mandy.

Mr Hope smiled at her. "Think," he said. "What do hens do at night?"

"Go to sleep?" said James.

"They roost," said Mandy. "They go to sleep on perches up off the ground so the foxes and rats can't harm them."

Mr Hope nodded. "Hens always roost at night," he said. "So if Ronda is going to come off the nest she'll come off at dusk when it's time to roost. If she stays on the nest the chances are she's broody. You could try her with the china eggs tonight if you're careful how you put them in."

"Can we stay and do that?" asked

Mandy. "Do we have to go now?"

"I'll tell you what," Mr Hope said. "I've got a few more calls to make. What if I collect you on my way home?"

"That would be great, Dad," Mandy said. "Thanks a lot."

"Do you think it'll work?" James asked.

Mr Masters shrugged. "It might," he said. "Some breeds make better broodies than others and Rhode Island Reds are usually pretty good. Just don't go giving Ronda a fright. You'll have to be very quiet down there."

"I'll pick you up later," Mr Hope said. "Be good."

Mandy and James waved goodbye to Mr Hope and ran down to the broody pen with the china eggs.

Mandy held her breath. Maybe Ronda was strutting around the scratching area again. But there was no sign of the Rhode Island Red as she and James rounded the corner of the barn.

"Shh," said James.

They peered into the pen. Libby was still there – and Ronda was still sitting on her nest.

Mandy hardly dared to breathe. Maybe it would work. The china eggs were warm in her hands. All they had to do now was make sure nothing disturbed Ronda before dusk. It would be agony waiting but it had to be done.

The sun had gone behind the barn and Mandy could hear the hens on the other nesting-boxes settling down for the night. There were faint rustlings and murmurings. Mandy and James sat quietly at the front of the pen. Libby was still in there with Ronda. The light was fading from the sky. Now was the moment. If Ronda went to roost, they had failed. Another half-hour or so and they would know.

"I'm hungry," James whispered. "Tea seems a long time ago."

"Just a while longer," Mandy whispered back.

There was a movement behind them and Libby appeared. Her eyes were shining.

"I think she's settled," she said. "She's been sitting on the same spot for ages. Should we try the eggs?"

Mandy and James looked at each other and nodded.

"*You'd* better do it," said Mandy to Libby. "You won't scare her."

"But I've never done it before," Libby said.

"You must've seen your dad do it," said James.

"Just slide them under her," Mandy said. "They're warm already. It's just to get her used to sitting on eggs."

Libby bit her lip. "OK, I'll try," she said.

She slipped back into the broody pen. Mandy and James heard her speaking softly to Ronda, soothing her, calming her. Mandy peered into the darkness. She saw Libby slip an egg under the hen's body. Ronda stirred and fluttered. Then she seemed to settle deeper into the nest. Libby turned to look at James and Mandy.

"Now the other one," Mandy whispered.

Libby took the other egg out of her pocket and very, very gently slipped it under Ronda. This time the hen barely stirred. Libby waited a moment then

slipped quietly out of the hen pen.

None of them spoke until they were right outside the pen. They stopped by the barn and looked back.

"Well done, Libby," Mandy said. "That was perfect."

"You didn't disturb her at all," James said.

Libby flushed with pleasure but her eyes were worried. "I hope she stays on the nest," she said.

Mandy and James nodded. "All we can do now is wait," Mandy said. "If she's still there in the morning the chances are she'll sit."

Libby looked at her. "The morning?" she said. "It's such a long time to wait."

"Just think of all the chicks Ronda is going to have," Mandy said. "That's worth waiting for, isn't it?"

Libby's eyes shone. "Oh, yes," she said. "That *is* worth waiting for!"

6

Success!

Mandy and James saw Libby in the playground first thing next morning. She was in the middle of a group of her classmates, all talking at once and asking her questions.

"She's still there," Libby said, running up to them. "Ronda is still on the nest."

"Libby is going to let us all see the chicks when they're hatched," said a little girl with bright-red hair.

"And you can come up to the farm and visit them, Nikki," Libby said.

"What about the rest of us?" said a dark-haired boy.

"You can all come, Tim," Libby said, looking round the little group. "All of you."

Mandy smiled. Libby had quite made up her mind that Ronda was going to have a whole brood of chicks.

"That's great," Mandy said. "But we've only put the *china* eggs in so far."

"When can we try real eggs?" James wanted to know.

Libby's face was glowing with excitement.

"Dad says we can try tonight," she said. "He thinks we should wait till dusk again, when she's settled for the night. That's the best time to try. You *will* be able to come, won't you? Mum said she would come and fetch you both after tea and take you home again later."

"Of course we'll come," said Mandy.

"Just you try and stop us!" James added.

The bell went and Libby dashed off with her friends.

"Libby is getting on really well with the rest of her class now," Mandy said.

James nodded. "Look at her!" he said. "She's got loads of friends."

Mandy smiled. "It looks like Libby's problem is solved," she said. "Now all we have to do is make sure Ronda has a brood of chicks to keep her company."

"Now all these eggs have a good chance of being fertile," Mr Masters said.

Mandy, James and Libby peered into the basket he was holding. Seven brown eggs nestled amongst the straw.

"Does that mean they'll turn into chicks?" Libby asked.

Mr Masters nodded. "If we're really lucky," he said. "We'll test them once

Ronda has been sitting on them for a little while, so don't be disappointed if one or two aren't fertile."

Libby looked at the eggs. "Just think," she said. "In three weeks' time they're all going to be chickens."

Mr Masters laughed. "In three weeks' time, if they all hatch out, they're going to be a lot of *work*. A real chick challenge. I hope you realise that!"

"Oh, we'll help," said Mandy.

"That's right," James said. "We know that young animals are always a lot of work. We don't mind."

Mr Masters raised his eyebrows. "I certainly hope so," he said. "It's going to keep Ronda busy, too."

"Ronda will love it," Libby said firmly. "I just know she will."

Mr Masters laughed again. "OK, then," he said. "Let's get started. First we'll get Ronda off the nest. Then we'll get the real eggs on it."

"But how do we do that?" asked Libby.

Mr Masters smiled. "She needs one good feed a day and a scratch-around," he said. "We can replace the eggs while she's feeding and with any luck she'll accept them."

Libby carried the tin dish of maize and corn carefully into the pen and put it down. Mandy fetched some water.

"Grain is the best feed for a sitting hen," Mr Masters said. "If you give her soft food, the droppings can foul the eggs."

"Couldn't you wash them?" James said.

Mr Masters shook his head. "Once she starts incubating the eggs you don't want to touch them any more than you have to," he said. "They can get cold very quickly and then they won't hatch out."

Libby tapped the side of the feed dish and there was a fluttering sound as Ronda flew down from the nest. She made for the food right away.

"OK, while she's busy with that you'd better get on with changing the eggs," Mr Masters said.

Mandy, Libby and James slipped into the pen and reached up to the nesting-box. Mandy scooped out the china eggs while James and Libby filled the nest with the real ones.

When they came back out Ronda was having a good long drink of water. They watched as she lifted her head and strutted over to a corner of the pen.

"What is she doing now?" asked Mandy.

"She's going to have a bath," Libby said. "She loves baths."

"What's she going to bath in?" asked James.

Libby giggled. "In the dust," she said. "Chickens always take dust-baths. It keeps their feathers clean."

James shook his head. "I wonder what Mum would say if *I* tried that," he said.

Mandy grinned. "She must be used to it," she said. "Blackie is always rolling in the dust."

Libby turned towards them. "Where

is Blackie?" she said. "You never bring him with you."

"We thought he might upset Ronda and the other chickens," James explained. "We wouldn't want to scare them."

Mr Masters nodded. "That's good thinking," he said. "It's easy for a hen to be scared off the nest, even by the friendliest of dogs."

Libby's mouth drooped. Then she cheered up. "Just wait till Ronda has her chicks," she said. "You can bring Blackie then. I'll bet he'll love them."

"Now," said Mr Masters, "let's see if Ronda will go back on the nest – and accept those eggs."

Mandy, Libby and James held their breath as Mr Masters picked Ronda up gently and put her back on her nest. Ronda ruffled her feathers and shifted her weight. Mr Masters came and stood beside the others.

"Just keep very still and watch," he said.

Ronda bent and poked at the nest with

her beak, shifting bits of straw, burrowing her feet and body into it, ruffling her feathers. Then she gave one last wriggle and settled down – and stayed absolutely still.

Mr Masters let out a low whistle and Mandy looked at him. "Well, I have to hand it to you," he said. "It looks as if you've done it. It looks as if Ronda's going to hatch those eggs after all."

The children looked at one another.

"I knew we could do it," Libby said,

her eyes shining. "I just *knew* it."

The sun had set now and the yard was deep in shadow. From all along the pen came the sounds of birds settling down for the night.

"Now we must leave her to get on with it," said Mr Masters. "It's up to Ronda now."

"But we have to look after her," Libby said.

"Indeed you do," said Mr Masters. "I've made out a list of all the things you have to do for your chick challenge. Come and have a look."

Mandy, James and Libby followed him into the house.

"There's your list," Mrs Masters said as she poured out juice for them and put a huge sponge cake on the kitchen table.

"Wow!" said James. "That cake looks brilliant."

"Help yourself." Mrs Masters smiled.

Mandy picked up the list and sat down at the table. "Look at this," she said. "We have to make sure Ronda gets plenty of grit to help her digest her food."

"That's important," said Mr Masters. "Hens don't have teeth and grit helps to grind their food up."

"And protein," said James, through a mouthful of cake.

Mr Masters nodded. "It might not seem like it, but it's hard work sitting on a nest for three weeks," he added. "She'll only be out for feeding and exercise once a day so it'll need to be a good feed."

"And what about afterwards, once the chicks are hatched?" Mandy asked.

"That's when the real work starts," Mr Masters said, smiling. "You won't get much peace then."

"Where are Ronda and her chicks going to live?" Libby asked.

"They could go into the coops with the other hens and chicks," said her mother.

Libby put her head on one side. "Wouldn't it be nice if Ronda had a little house of her own?" she asked.

Mr Masters ran a hand through his hair. "I'm sorry, Libby," he said. "I just don't have time at the moment for building a new coop."

Mandy looked up. "I know somebody who would do it," she said. "And we could help him."

"Who?" said Libby.

Mandy grinned. "Grandad," she said. "He made a rabbit hutch for Jack Gardiner. I'm sure he could make a hen coop."

"That would be brilliant," Libby said. "When can we ask him?"

"Are you sure he wouldn't mind?" Mrs Masters asked Mandy.

James laughed. "He won't," he said. "Mandy's grandad is used to it – so is her gran. They're great at helping out."

"That *would* be kind," said Mr Masters. "But you mustn't put your grandad to too much trouble, Mandy."

"He'd love to make a special house just for Ronda and her family," Mandy said.

"A special house for a special hen," said James.

Libby nibbled on a large slice of sponge cake. "Isn't it lovely? Ronda is going to have a whole family of chicks!"

7

A house for Ronda

"And you'll help us, Grandad?" Mandy said.

Grandad looked at Mandy, Libby and James.

"As if I had any choice!" he said with a twinkle in his eye. "Of course I'll help you. But I'll need a picture of a hen coop.

I'm not sure I know what's needed."

"Oh, that's all right," Mandy said. "I've brought a book."

"And Dad made some drawings," Libby added.

Gran laughed out loud. "It's nice to see that you came prepared. While you're looking at that book, I'll put the kettle on."

"Good idea," said Grandad. He was already studying the drawing Libby had brought.

By the time Gran had brought the tea out into the garden, Grandad was making a list.

"We'll get the wood from Fenton's timberyard," he said. "And we'll need some chicken wire. I think I've got some roofing felt in the garage already."

"When can we start?" Mandy asked as Gran handed round tea.

Grandad took a mug of tea and dived into the biscuit barrel. "Mmm," he said. "Ginger biscuits. My favourite."

"Grandad!" Mandy said.

"Tomorrow is Saturday," he said. "Be here bright and early and we'll start then."

"We'll be here," said James.

"And I'll get my dad to bring me," said Libby.

"Just look how much we've done in two days," James said on Sunday afternoon.

Mandy pushed her fair hair out of her eyes and looked at their handiwork. The coop was just like a little wooden house. The roof was covered in roofing felt. There was a small opening at one side and a sliding door at the other.

"We've still to do the run," Grandad said.

James smiled. "When it's finished it'll look just like a tiny house with a front garden," he said.

"It looks terrific," Libby said. "Ronda is going to be so pleased."

"How is she?" Mandy asked.

"Dad says she's doing really well,"

Libby answered. "He's going to test the eggs this week. Do you want to come and see?"

"Sure," said James. "When is he going to do it?"

"Thursday, I think," Libby said. "He has to do it while Ronda is out for her exercise."

"I reckon this coop should be finished by Thursday," Grandad said. "Why don't I take you up to the farm and we can deliver it then?"

"Brilliant," said Mandy. "Can we start on the run?"

Grandad laughed. "All right. Just let me finish my tea break!"

It was quite late when they finished fitting the frame of the run together and tacked on the chicken wire. The run *was* like a little garden in front of the coop, as James said – a place for Ronda and her chicks to scratch about in and get some exercise.

"Just the top to do now," said Grandad.

"Top?" said James.

Grandad nodded. "You have to put a mesh lid on top of the run to keep out vermin like rats and foxes," he said.

"Are we going to do that now?" asked Mandy.

Grandad shook his head. "It's too late," he said. "But I'll have it done by Thursday, don't you worry." He looked at the coop. "I could never have got on this fast without you three."

Mandy, James and Libby grinned at one another.

"It was great fun," said Libby. Her eyes lit up. "Do you think we could paint it once we get it to the farm?"

"That's a brilliant idea," said Mandy. "What colour?"

Libby thought for a moment. Then she giggled. "Red, of course," she said. "Because Ronda is a Rhode Island Red."

Mr and Mrs Masters thought the coop was terrific too.

"I should get you to come up and make a few more of those for me," Mr Masters joked, as he and Grandad stood looking down at it. "It was really good of you to take the time to do it."

"It was a pleasure," Grandad said. "Now, where is this famous Ronda that I've heard so much about?"

Mr Masters led the way to the broody pen.

"There she is," Libby whispered.

"Time for her daily feed and exercise," Mr Masters said.

Mandy, James and Libby fetched the food and water, but Ronda didn't seem to want to move.

"Rhode Island Reds are such good broodies," Mr Masters said. "Sometimes it's hard to get them off the nest once they've decided to sit."

Libby went very softly up to Ronda and lifted her down from the nest. "There," she said. "Have your dinner and your drink."

"And don't forget your bath, Ronda," James added.

Mandy looked at Mr Masters. He had a torch in one hand.

"I'm going to candle the eggs now," he said to her.

Mandy looked puzzled. "Candle?" she repeated.

"Watch," Mr Masters said.

Libby, Mandy, James and Grandad all gathered round. It was getting quite dark now.

Mr Masters picked an egg out of the nest and held it between his thumb and forefinger. "Gather closer," he said. "We want to cut out all the light we can."

They moved closer together, hardly breathing as Mr Masters switched on the powerful torch and held it behind the egg.

"Look," he said. "This one is fertile."

Mandy looked, but all she could see was a big dark patch inside the egg and a small clear area at the thick end of the shell.

"What's that dark patch?" she asked.

Mr Masters switched off the light. "That's the chicken," he said, smiling.

"What?" said Mandy in amazement. "Can we see it again?"

Mr Masters put the egg back and picked up another. Again he switched on the torch and Mandy looked carefully. There, inside the eggshell, was the dark patch which would develop into a chicken.

"That's incredible," said James as

Mr Masters replaced that egg and took another.

This time the torchlight shone clear through the shell.

"What does that mean?" Mandy asked.

"I'm afraid there's no chicken inside that one," Mr Masters said. "It's infertile."

"Oh, what a pity," Libby said.

Mandy leaned over, eager to see if there was a chicken inside the next one. "Why did you say you were going to 'candle' them?" she asked.

Mr Masters smiled. "Because before torches were invented farmers had to do this with a candle," he said.

"Oh, right," said Mandy. "That one has a chicken inside."

"Would you like to try it?" Mr Masters asked.

Mandy looked at him in the torchlight. "May I?"

"Of course," Mr Masters replied. "Go ahead, pick up an egg."

Mandy reached into the nest and lifted

out a brown egg. "Oh," she said. "I'd forgotten they would be warm."

"Now hold it carefully," Mr Masters said. "I'll shine the torch for you."

Mandy held the egg between her thumb and forefinger, as he had done.

"Not too tightly," Mr Masters said. Then he switched on the light.

Mandy looked at the egg. "Fertile," she said happily. "Just think. I'm holding a tiny little chicken inside an egg. It's wonderful!"

Mr Masters swivelled the torch round so that it was pointing at the nest and Mandy replaced the egg. There were two more eggs: one fertile, one infertile.

"That's pretty good," Mr Masters said. "Five out of seven is a very good average."

"Five chicks," said Libby. "Oh, I can hardly wait another whole week!"

"Time to get Ronda back on the nest, I think," Mr Masters said. "We don't want these eggs getting cold."

Libby carried Ronda in and she settled back happily on her nest.

"Will she notice that two eggs are missing?" Libby asked.

Mr Masters shook his head. "I don't think so," he said.

"That's good," said Libby. "Everybody at school is going to be so excited. Five chicks! I just can't wait to tell them!"

8

Eggs in danger

Mr Hope took Mandy and James up to Blackheath Farm the following weekend to paint the coop.

"I'm going to put a notice on the bulletin board at school every day," Libby said. "Everybody wants to know about Ronda and the chick challenge –

especially now there are only a few days to go."

James dipped his brush in the pot of red paint. "I think that's a great idea," he said.

Mandy smiled. Libby was making lots of friends now that all her classmates were interested in Ronda.

"How are Nikki and Tim?" she asked.

"They want to adopt a chick each once they're hatched," Libby said.

"Do they want to keep them as pets?" Mandy asked.

Libby shook her head. "Oh, no," she said. "I wouldn't want Ronda to lose any of her chicks. But Tim and Nikki can come here and see them every week. The chicks will be their special ones. They're already thinking up names for them."

"What about the rest of the chicks?" said James.

Libby put her head on one side. "Laura and Jack would like to adopt one as well," she said. "And Susan Davis. In fact everybody would like a special chick."

"You won't have enough to go round," said Mandy.

"Oh, that's all right," Libby said. "Ronda is sure to have more chicks – enough for everybody."

Mandy laughed. "Ronda *is* going to be busy. It's lucky she's got such a nice coop."

James looked at the coop. "You know, it looks so good it should have a name. Just like a proper house," he said.

"What? Like Blackheath Farm?" said Libby.

"Or Animal Ark?" added Mandy.

James nodded and his face lit up.

"That's what we need," he said. "A sign – like the Animal Ark sign."

"With the name on it," said Libby.

"But what would you call it?" said Mandy.

"How about Chicken Cottage?" James suggested.

"Or Hen House," added Libby.

"I know," Mandy said. "Ronda's Residence."

"What does 'residence' mean?" Libby asked.

"It's a posh name for a house," James explained.

Libby giggled. "That's OK then," she said. "Ronda is posh, too."

"So what we need is a post and a board," Mandy said.

"Dad is sure to have some wood somewhere," Libby said. "Let's go and ask him."

They found Mr Masters mending a fence in the farmyard near the broody pen. Ronda was the only broody left now. All the other hens had hatched their chicks.

"I've got just what you need," he said. "Come on. I'll cut it to the right size for you."

They followed Mr Masters into the barn and watched while he got the wood out of the store and measured it. Then he cut it, smoothed the edges and gave it to them.

"You paint it and then I'll put it up for you," he said. "And remember: nice neat lettering." He picked up a wooden pole. "This should do for a post," he added.

"How do you spell 'residence'?" Libby asked.

Mandy grinned. "Maybe we'll just call it Ronda's Range," she said. "After all, she is a free-range chicken."

"That's a good idea," said Libby. "Ronda's Range!"

Suddenly there was a commotion outside. Libby turned, her face anxious. "That's Ronda!" she said. "Something's happened."

Before anybody could stop her, Libby was out of the door and racing towards the broody pen.

Mr Masters was right behind her, still carrying the pole. Mandy and James followed. They rounded the corner of the barn and stopped dead in their tracks.

"Go away! Go away!" Libby was yelling.

The Rhode Island Red was running round in front of the broody pen, squawking and flapping her wings.

Then Mandy saw what Libby was shouting at. It was a fox. Mr Masters scooped Libby up with one hand and thrust her behind him.

"Hold on to her," he said to Mandy, "and stay back. A cornered fox is dangerous."

Mandy hugged Libby and held on tight. Libby wriggled in her grasp. "The fox. It'll get Ronda! It'll get the eggs!" she cried, tears streaming down her face.

"No it won't," said James. "Look!"

Libby looked up. Mr Masters walked towards the fox and threw the wooden post. Mandy gasped, then she saw that he hadn't thrown the pole to hurt the fox, but just to frighten it. The fox jumped sideways and, quick as a flash,

streaked through the hole in the fence
and out into the open fields beyond.

"It's all right now. It's gone," Mandy
said to Libby.

But Libby was still crying. "Ronda!"
she cried and ran towards her. But
Ronda was too upset. She continued to
run around, flapping her wings.

"Leave her for a moment," Mr Masters
said. "Give her time to calm down."

But Ronda didn't calm down. She
wouldn't even let Libby pick her up at

first and when she eventually did she certainly wouldn't let the little girl put her back on the nest. She wriggled and fluttered and wouldn't settle.

"The eggs," Mandy said. "What are we going to do about the eggs?"

Mr Masters looked at his watch. "We'll have to do something soon," he said. "If we leave it much longer the eggs will get cold."

"And then they won't hatch," added Libby. "Oh, that bad fox."

Mandy gave her a hug. "It wasn't the fox's fault," she said. "That's the way they're made. It's just their nature."

"It's my fault," Mr Masters said. "If I'd mended that fence the fox wouldn't have got in."

"But you were helping us instead," said James.

Mr Masters smiled. "OK," he said. "It's nobody's fault. But we still have a problem to solve. Come on, I need your help."

Mandy and James followed Mr Masters into the hay barn while Libby tried to calm Ronda. Mr Masters picked up a wooden box and pointed to a pile of hay.

"You two fill the box," he said. "I'll go and get the eggs."

Mandy and James didn't ask any questions. Mr Masters was obviously in a hurry. He was back in no time, with Ronda's eggs carefully laid on straw on the bottom of a basket.

"Now, if you can make a hollow in that hay," he said, "I'll put the eggs in."

Mandy scooped out a handful of hay and pressed the rest down.

"Is this to keep the eggs warm?" James asked.

Mr Masters nodded. "It's called a haybox," he said. "Farmers used to use them all the time before they had incubators. The hay keeps the eggs warm."

"I've heard of hayboxes," said Mandy. "But I thought they were for cooking."

Mr Masters smiled. "In the old days people used them for cooking too," he said. "If you put a hot casserole in here it would keep on cooking for hours."

"It won't cook the eggs, though, will it?" said James, alarmed.

Mr Masters shook his head. "No," he said. "It only *preserves* the heat. It'll just keep the eggs nicely warm."

He lifted the eggs very gently out of the basket and placed them carefully in amongst the hay.

"We can't keep them in here too long," he said. "But if we can keep them warm enough and get Ronda back on to the nest, we might have a chance."

Mandy covered the eggs over with more hay. "How long have we got?" she asked.

Mr Masters shrugged. "I wouldn't like to risk more than a few hours," he said. "I've heard of people keeping eggs warm a lot longer than that, but it's a big risk."

Mandy bit her lip. "Libby will calm Ronda down," she said. "You'll see."

Mr Masters packed more hay into the box and put it safely up on a shelf in the barn.

"Come on," he said. "Let's see how she's getting on."

Libby was sitting in the dust with Ronda beside her. The Rhode Island Red was a lot calmer; she wasn't running around any more. But she was pecking nervously at the grass and scratching in the dirt.

"She won't go back," Libby said softly.

Mr Masters kept his voice low. "Give her time," he said. "Don't rush her."

It was the hardest thing. Mandy wanted to lift Ronda up and put her back on the nest but she knew that would be the wrong thing to do. It would be even worse if Ronda started to sit on her eggs and then got off the nest again.

Libby sat in the dirt beside Ronda, singing to her in a low voice. The hen began to scratch at the dirt less and less, and moved closer to the little girl. Libby reached out a hand and smoothed Ronda's ruffled feathers. Slowly, step by step, Ronda came and pressed herself close to Libby. Libby gathered her up in her arms and rocked her, still singing softly.

Mandy and James looked at each other and smiled. It was amazing to watch Ronda growing calmer and calmer.

"I think you could try now," Mr Masters said softly.

Libby didn't even turn round. She stood up carefully and carried Ronda over to the nest where she gently put her down. Ronda fluttered her wings and for an awful moment Mandy thought the hen was going to fly off. Then Ronda wriggled around and settled down. Libby backed away.

"We'll have to leave her for a while," Mr Masters said. "Just to make sure she's settled. We can't risk putting the eggs back until we're sure she's going to stay there."

"How long do we have to wait?" Libby asked.

Mr Masters ruffled her hair. "I'll try putting them back tonight," he said. "Hens always settle better at night. We'll know in the morning if she's going to stay."

"But we won't know if the eggs are harmed?" said Mandy.

Mr Masters frowned. "We won't know for certain," he said. "Not until the weekend. The eggs should start hatching by then. Meanwhile, we'll just have to hope for the best."

"But they just *have* to be all right," Libby said desperately. "Ronda *can't* lose her chicks now — not after keeping them warm and safe for so long. And what about Nikki and Tim? I've *promised* they can adopt a chick."

Mr Masters bent down and gave her a hug. "We've done the best we can,

Libby," he said. "You did a great job getting Ronda back on to the nest."

Mandy bit her lip. "And remember what you said, Libby. Ronda can have other chicks."

Libby's eyes filled with tears. "But it won't be the same," she said. "They won't be *these* chicks. They won't be her very first chicks."

9

Easter Party

Mandy and James were throwing a stick for Blackie in the back garden of Animal Ark on Saturday morning when the telephone rang.

"Mandy!" Mrs Hope called. "It's Libby for you. She sounds excited."

They looked at each other.

"It must be the chicks," James said.

Mandy nodded. "The eggs are due for hatching." She raced for the telephone.

James stood beside her as she took the call. Blackie tugged at his sleeve. The Labrador wanted to get back to their game.

"They've started to hatch!" Mandy said to James and her mum. Then she spoke into the phone. "Of course we'll come. Just as soon as we can. See you, Libby. Bye!"

"How many chicks have hatched?" James asked.

Mandy smiled. "Just one so far."

"Let's get up there fast," said James. Then he looked dismayed. "But how?"

Mrs Hope laughed. "Oh, I can think of a way!" she said. "I'll take you. And don't worry about missing anything, James. Eggs take a long time to hatch out. You'll be there all day if you wait until they're all hatched. You'd better phone your mum, and let her know where you're going."

"What about Blackie?" James said.

"We can take him, can't we, Mum?" Mandy asked.

Mrs Hope bent down and gave Blackie a pat. The Labrador looked up at her and wagged his tail.

"Just make sure he doesn't frighten Ronda," she said. "Now, are we going up to Blackheath or not?"

"You bet we are," Mandy answered, racing for the door.

But at the back of her mind there was still a worry. Were all the eggs OK? Had some of them got chilled? Would Ronda manage to hatch out all of her chicks?

"Oh, look," said Mandy softly. "Isn't it beautiful?"

The children looked in wonder at the tiny little chick as it started to emerge from the eggshell. First there was just the tiniest crack in the shell. Then the point of a beak appeared, chipping at the shell, making the hole bigger. Then a downy golden head appeared. Its bright, beady eyes blinked in the light as it looked around and its yellow coat glistened.

Ronda looked down and wriggled her body, raising her wing slightly. The chick scrabbled at the sides of its shell and, with an enormous effort, scrambled out of it altogether. For a moment it stood there uncertainly, a tiny yellow bundle. Then it scampered under Ronda's wing and the hen settled her feathers around it.

"How many does that make?" asked James.

"Three," Libby said. She peered at the nest, trying to see the chicks cuddled close under Ronda's body.

"I can hear another one tapping at the shell," James said, his ear close to the nest.

"That can go on for ages," Mandy said. "Don't you feel like giving the poor little thing a helping hand."

Libby shook her head. "Dad says the mother hen knows what to do. It's best to leave the eggs alone."

"Why don't we go and put the finishing touches to Ronda's Range?" said James.

They found Mr Masters in the back garden of the farmhouse. He was fixing the sign to the hen coop.

"Hello, there," he said. "I just thought I'd get this ready. We should be able to transfer Ronda and her chicks to it tonight. How is she getting on?"

"Three hatched out so far," Mandy said. She looked at the coop. "That looks great, Mr Masters."

Ronda's coop looked really bright with its red paint. Mr Masters hung the notice on the post over the door. It said *Ronda's Range*.

"That's nearly as good as the Animal Ark sign," said James.

"I thought we'd set it up near the house for tonight," Mr Masters said. "We'll put it in the back garden so we can keep an eye on Ronda and her chicks."

Mandy, James and Libby helped Mr Masters to get Ronda's new home ready. Blackie was very interested in what was going on.

"Get down, Blackie," James said. "It's not for you. It's for Ronda."

They put a thick layer of paper on the floor of the coop, checked the wire netting and put the dust tray down in one corner.

"Once the coop is out in the yard they can have a proper dust-bath," Mr Masters said. "But a tray of sand and earth will do for now."

"Here's the grit box," James said.

"And don't forget the water," Mr Masters added. "We can put the food out later."

"That's perfect," said Libby as they looked at their handiwork.

Mandy frowned. "Won't the chicks be cold?" she asked. "They're so tiny."

"Don't you worry about that," Mr Masters said. "Even day-old chicks are pretty tough. And, don't forget, they've got Ronda to keep them warm. Right – time for tea!"

Mandy remembered the chicks snuggled under Ronda's warm body. It must be really cosy tucked up amongst all those feathers, she thought.

"No wonder they use feathers for quilts," she said out loud, as they went in for tea. She looked back at the coop.

Soon Ronda and her little brood would be in their new home.

It was almost dark by the time all the chicks were hatched. Mandy, James and Libby waited while Mr Masters checked them. He turned to them, smiling.

"I must say you lot have done a great job here," he said. "All five of the eggs have hatched – and they're all fine healthy chicks."

"So the haybox worked," said Mandy. "They didn't get chilled."

"It's been a real success," Mr Masters said. "Now, who's going to help me move them?"

Mandy and James filled a box with fresh hay and scooped out a hollow.

"That should do," Mr Masters said. He looked at Libby. "OK," he said, "you can lift Ronda now."

Mandy reached for the Rhode Island Red and gathered her into her arms. Mandy and James stared at the chicks, fascinated. The little creatures scuttled about as the cool air struck them. Then Mr Masters began scooping them up in his hands and transferring them to the box Mandy and James held between them.

"Now put Ronda back," he said. Libby settled the hen back on her chicks.

"Poor little things," Mandy said. "They must be wondering what's happening to them."

"They'll soon be in their nice new home," Mr Masters reassured her, as they made their way towards the farmhouse.

Mrs Masters was waiting for them. Blackie was with her.

"I've put out a good feed for Ronda," she said. "She'll need it after all her hard work."

Ronda thought so too. As soon as Mr Masters put her into the run she made for the feed dish. The chicks scampered after her, tucking themselves close around her. Blackie peered into the run, snuffling at the little yellow bodies.

"Aren't they lovely, Blackie?" James said. "Absolutely perfect!"

The light spilled out of the back door of the farmhouse as they stood around the coop, watching Ronda and her chicks.

"Wonderful," Libby said softly. "I can't wait to tell everybody at school."

Mandy smiled. Ronda was totally caught up in her little family. She was going to be a very busy hen for a while, and wouldn't have time to mope any more.

And Libby had made friends too. She wouldn't miss Ronda while she was at school now. Her friends were just as interested in Ronda and her chicks as Libby was. It really did look as if everything had worked out perfectly.

"You know," said James. "Ronda is going to steal the show at the Easter Party."

"What?" said Libby.

James looked at her. "You haven't forgotten, have you?" he said. "I'm taking Blackie, and Laura and Jack are taking their rabbits. I thought you were taking Ronda."

"And her chicks," added Mandy.

Libby's face lit up. "I *had* forgotten," she said. She turned to her father. "Can I, Dad?" she asked. "May I take Ronda and the chicks to the Easter Party?"

Mr Masters laughed. "That's three weeks away," he said. "I reckon Ronda's chicks will be big and strong enough to stand the excitement – if you look after them."

"Oh, we will," said Libby. "Really we will!"

"Happy Easter!" Mandy called to Mrs McFarlane as they passed the post-office window on their way to the fancy dress party at school.

Mrs McFarlane waved from behind an enormous display of Easter eggs.

"Happy Easter!" Mr Hardy called back, coming out of the door of the Fox and Goose.

The whole of Welford Primary School was marching down the main street to show off their Easter costumes and masks. They were carrying baskets of Easter eggs they had collected from all the shops and houses in the village for the cottage hospital.

The school always donated Easter eggs to the hospital. Gary Roberts had been in hospital one Easter and he said it was the best Easter ever – he got so many chocolate eggs!

Mandy looked around her. Blackie was wearing a huge yellow ribbon round his neck. Laura and Jack were carrying a big wicker basket between them, and inside it their Easter bunnies were decked out in pink and blue ribbons.

Mandy moved towards Richard Tanner. "How's Duchess?" she asked.

"She's almost back to normal now," Richard said. "I don't think you'd even notice the limp if you didn't know about it."

Mandy smiled. "And what about the kittens?" she said.

"Beautiful!" Richard said. "We've got homes for all of them. You know, if Duchess hadn't had the kittens to look after, I don't think she would have recovered so quickly."

Mandy nodded. "That's what Dad said."

"I mean, she would have been really miserable," Richard said. "But the kittens cheered her up."

Mandy looked at Libby. She, Nikki

and Tim were pushing a wheelbarrow full of straw and in the middle of it were Ronda and her chicks.

"Aren't they gorgeous?" James said.

Mandy nodded. Libby looked over and waved.

"It's so wonderful," she called. "All Ronda's chicks have been adopted."

Mandy waved back. What a great Easter present, she thought. Chicks for Ronda. Chums for Libby. And chick chums for Libby's friends. Perfect! The chick challenge had had a very happy ending.

Read more about Animal Ark in
Pony Parade

1

James on holiday

"Come on, Blackie," Mandy said. She smiled down at the young Labrador and tugged gently on his lead. "We'll have to turn round and go back now. They'll be waiting for you!"

Blackie wagged his tail and carried on snuffling at the grass verge. "Come *on!*"

Mandy said more firmly. "You've sniffed enough to last for hours. Besides, here's James coming to fetch us," she added as she saw her best friend running down the lane.

"Hurry up, Mandy," James called. "We're almost ready to leave."

Blackie looked up at the sound of James's voice. Then, barking joyfully, he tugged Mandy off towards him.

"Well, *that* got him moving!" Mandy chuckled, handing Blackie's lead to James.

"Good job too," James said. "Mum and Dad are just loading the last lot of stuff into the car. Gosh, Mandy, there are so many bags. You'd think we were going for a month, not just three days!"

Just then Blackie started pulling at the lead and James groaned. "Not that way, Blackie. Back home quickly, boy. Dad won't want to be kept waiting. Oh, help!" he added. "Now he's wound his lead round my legs."

Mandy bent down to unwind the

lead. As soon as she'd done it, Blackie jumped up at her and nearly knocked her over. "What a pest you are, Blackie," she said lovingly. "Now, get walking!"

"That's what he was like before you came and took him out," James said as, at last, Blackie started walking in the right direction. "Getting in everyone's way, tripping us up or almost knocking us over. *And* he kept pulling things out of boxes and running off with them."

"He probably thought he was helping," Mandy chuckled.

"That's what *I* said," James told her. "But Mum and Dad didn't agree."

"Poor Blackie," Mandy said, bending to stroke him. Blackie sat down suddenly and James almost fell over him.

"Whoops!" Mandy laughed. "Sorry, James. That was my fault."

They straightened themselves out and started walking again.

"Here you are," said Mr Hunter as they reached the car. "You've been so long I thought you'd taken Blackie home, Mandy. I imagined you'd decided to keep him with you while *we* went on holiday," he joked. The Hunters were having a long weekend in the Lake District.

"I wish I could," Mandy replied. "I'm really going to miss him." She bent to give the Labrador a final pat. Then James put him in the back of the car, behind the special dog guard.

"*I'm* going to miss Benji," James said. "Look, he's sitting on the wall, watching. I'm sure he's upset about being left behind."

"James! If you don't get in, we'll leave *you* behind as well," said Mrs Hunter, popping her head out of the car window. "Stop worrying about Benji. He'll be fine with Mrs Padgett looking after him."

Mrs Padgett was the Hunters' next-door neighbour. She loved cats and Benji was very fond of her.

"Yes, I suppose you're right," James said as he scrambled into the car. "OK, Dad. I'm ready!"

"Bye, James!" Mandy called as the car set off. "Have a great time. I'll see you in three days!"

Mandy waved until the car turned the corner. Then she turned to look at Benji. She was just in time to see his tail disappearing round the side of Mrs Padgett's house. So Benji didn't seem to mind about being left behind, after all!

ANIMAL Action ™

RSPCA

If you like *Animal Ark*® then you'll love *Animal Action*! Subscribe for just **£8** and you can look forward to six issues of *Animal Action* magazine, throughout the year. Each issue of *Animal Action* is bursting with animal news and features, competitions and fun and games! Plus, when you subscribe, you'll become a free *Animal Action* Club member too, so we'll send you a fab joining pack and FREE donkey notepad and pen!

To subscribe, simply complete the form below – a photocopy is fine – and send it with a cheque for £8 (made payable to RSPCA) to RSPCA Animal Action Club, Wilberforce Way, Southwater, Horsham, West Sussex RH13 9RS.

Don't delay, join today!

Name:

Address:

Postcode:	Date of birth:

Signature of parent/guardian: